DEAD MAN'S RETURN

A terrible fear paralyses Leyton, Texas. On the morning Sheriff Jack Anderson is to hang an innocent youth for horse theft, Jim Jackson arrives, searching for the man who betrayed him and sent him to hell for ten years. Is Anderson that man? How can Jackson exact revenge in a town full of cold-blooded and desperate killers? And just how far along the trail of violence can a good man walk before he becomes as bad as those he is hunting?

DEREK RUTHERFORD

◆

DEAD MAN'S RETURN

Complete and Unabridged

LINFORD
Leicester

First published in Great Britain in 2018 by
Robert Hale
an imprint of The Crowood Press
Wiltshire

First Linford Edition
published 2022
by arrangement with The Crowood Press
Wiltshire

A catalogue record for this book is available
from the British Library.

ISBN 978-1-4448-4856-4

Published by
Ulverscroft Limited
Anstey, Leicestershire

Printed and bound in Great Britain by
TJ Books Ltd., Padstow, Cornwall

This book is printed on acid-free paper

1

Charles Beecher and Washington Smith built their saw mill four miles west of the Georgetown boundary line. They funded a spur from the main railroad line into the saw mill yard. The spur split into several sidings. There was a switch system that allowed locomotives that brought in virgin lumber to be moved to the far end of the train ready to haul out the flatbeds loaded with cut wood. A long platform was constructed alongside the track. Small cranes lifted the timbers from the wagons and swung them over into a holding pond, from where they were floated down to the saw mill. Three huge stationary engines were installed at the mill. The engines pulled the heavy logs from the water, dragged them up to one of six cutting rows, and also drove the huge circular saw blades. Beyond the stationary engines was a small section of railroad track on which horse-pulled wagons brought coal up to the engines. A smaller steam engine ran a water pump, sucking water in from the river over three miles away through a series of clay pipes. It felt like there was always a locomotive somewhere in the yard, belching smoke and hissing, clanking and grinding, either having just brought in coal or timber, or readying to take out the cut wood. The stationary engines ran from dawn until dusk, sometimes well into the night, pumping smoke and steam into the air. Saw blades screeched and sparked as they cut through hard wood. Horses neighed and cried, and over a hundred men yelled and laughed and argued. The sound of shovels and picks, cranes and hammers rang out on the warm still air. The cook's ovens and fire-pits burned ceaselessly. The yard's own blacksmith had a forge roaring day and night. There were bunk-houses, and offices, stables and workshops, latrines and wash-houses. There was an on-site tavern with its own rather large whiskey still alongside over two dozen fermenting barrels of beer out back, and a piano in front. Beecher and Smith had their own telegraph office with the cables running alongside the railway tracks.

Four miles had felt plenty far enough all those years ago when Beecher and Smith had started the mill. It wasn't that they cared for the sensibilities of the townsfolk. It was simply that such distance meant they were less likely to face issues and complaints. The fact that Georgetown was now expanding towards the mill wasn't their issue. The mill had been there first, the two men would argue. You want to build a house nearby, that's your choice. But don't do so and then moan about the noise.

These days they had a bigger issue.

It was two months since Jim Jackson had sprung Leon Winters from a prison leasing camp a hundred miles north.

Beecher was in Smith's plush office overlooking the mill site.

'What's this fellow's name?' Beecher said.

'Abraham,' Smith said.

'Abraham what?'

'No idea. He's simply known as Abraham. Actually he's known as the Tall Man.'

'The Tall Man?'

'I guess he's tall.'

'And he's good?'

'The best. So I'm told.'

Beecher pulled a watch from his vest pocket. It was a quarter of ten.

'What time will he be here?'

'Ten o'clock.'

'I'm still not convinced this is advisable.' Beecher was tall, himself. Thin, too. And his hair was greying.

Smith sighed. 'Look at all of this.' He swept an arm out in front of him, taking in not just the room, but the entire mill site beyond the panelled wooden walls. 'Think of your house in Austin. Your *mansion*. Mary. The kids. Everything. You want to risk it?'

'But there's no guarantee that Jackson and Winters are going after him.'

'Wouldn't you? Think about it, man.'

Beecher didn't need to think about it.

He'd done nothing but think about it ever since he'd heard about the Leon Winters prison break. A man named Jack Anderson, who turned out to be vicious and cruel, and maybe even crazy, was up in a town called Leyton running the place like it was his own little empire. It was Jack Anderson who had framed Leon Winters and Jim Jackson and had put them behind bars for ten years. Beecher had no idea whether or not Winters and Jackson knew of Jack Anderson. Indeed how would they know? Anderson wasn't even the man's real name. But *if* they did know of him, it made sense that they would go after him. And *if* they did . . . and if he talked . . . then the trail might lead right back here. It was why Smith was so keen to get rid of Jack Anderson. Many times over the years Smith had proposed the idea to Beecher. *Getting shot of a loose end*, was how Smith always described it. Beecher had always reined him in. *There's no point*, he'd argue. *Let sleeping dogs lie.* But now things were different.

'I thought they'd have caught Winters

5

and Jackson by now,' Smith said. 'But they haven't. It's been two months.'

'I believe there are Texas Rangers in Leyton,' Beecher said. 'To get to Anderson Winters and Jackson have to go to Leyton, and if they go there the Rangers will catch them.'

'The Rangers have gone. *If* they ever were there. They supposedly waited six weeks. Nothing. So they've pulled out. I'm not sure we weren't told a pack of lies about them,'

'Anyway, how would Winters and Jackson even know where to find Anderson?'

'I've no idea. But is that a risk you're happy to take?'

Smith again held out his hands, illustrating what they could lose.

'It's tenuous,' Beecher said. The thing was they weren't even sure that Anderson knew who *they* were. Nevertheless, he and Smith had had the debate many times over the years. He knew this time he wouldn't win.

The jailbreak had changed things.

Anderson might be able to link him and Smith to a killing that had, indirectly, helped the two of them to all of this, the mill, the mansions, the money, the lifestyle they enjoyed. If Winters and Jackson got to Anderson, and extracted the truth, then what next?

There was a knock on the office door.

'Come in,' Smith said.

The door opened and Evelyn, the secretary, peered round. She was a pretty red-head and Beecher wasn't sure but had always wondered if Washington Smith wasn't employing her for more than just her business skills.

'There's a man to see you both,' she said, smiling. 'Abraham. Didn't give a second name.'

'Send him in,' Smith said.

Abraham was quite possibly the tallest man that Beecher had ever seen. He was holding a black hat and was wearing a long dark coat. He had a beard that reached halfway down his chest and he wore two guns.

He waited until Evelyn had closed the

7

door then he said, 'Gentlemen. I believe you want somebody killed.'

2

Leon Winters coughed quietly into his hand so as not to wake the lovers. They were huddled together beneath a blanket on the far side of the low fire. It was bittersweet, the way they were. He was happy for them — so very happy — and he was equally happy to be free. He owed that freedom to Jim Jackson and knew it was a debt he could never repay. Yet their loving brought back hard and painful memories that he had long buried. His wife Charlotte and their son Harvey had succumbed to tuberculosis that many years ago he couldn't count. It was one of the reasons he'd ended up robbing trains and, ultimately, doing prison time. Hell, it was the *only* reason. If Charlotte and Harvey had lived then everything would have been different. Looking at Jim and Rosalie, not just now, but over the last two months, seeing them grow closer, become lovers, watching them find that magic that is offered but once in a life-time, made him sad for his own loss, whilst being as happy as a man could be for his friends.

He coughed quietly again. His lungs hurt and he felt something splatter against his hands. He shuffled closer to the fire and held out his palms to the flickering light.

Blood.

It was how it had started with Charlotte, and again with Harvey. A little breathlessness, a cough, some pain, and then blood.

So they did kill me, he thought. All those years, those desperately terrible years. They'd mistreated him, starved him, beat him, froze him, tied him up in the blazing sun, and tried to goad him into running just so they could shoot him down. All those years in which he had fought every day to survive simply to deny them the pleasure of his death. All that and when he was finally free — thanks to Jim — it turned out that he was dying anyway.

So be it. Dying, too, was bittersweet. He would see Charlotte and Harvey on the other side. But in the meantime he and Jim and Rosalie had something they had to do. And he would be there and make sure it happened, make sure they were safe.

They had a future.

Below them, if he walked to the edge of the trees and looked out across the plain, the faint lights of Leyton could be seen. Oil lamps in saloon windows, a fire — maybe rubbish — burning on the edge of town. Tomorrow they would ride down there. The man they were searching for — Jack Anderson — reputedly ran the town. The question was, would Jack Anderson turn out to be John Allan, the only other member of their old gang who was still alive? The only one who didn't appear to have done prison time.

They'd talked through the events of that day — their last train robbery — numerous times in the last few months as they recuperated from the wounds sustained in the prison break, trying to make sense of the killing, seeing if there was anything they had missed, running it by Rosalie on the off-chance a fresh pair of eyes might spot something new.

But it always came out the same.

It always pointed to John Allan.

Leon himself had been on the driver plate that day, holding a gun on the engineer and fireman. He'd seen nothing of what had happened. All he knew was hearsay, but he'd heard it so many times and from so many people that it felt like he'd been right there in the carriage where the man was shot.

They'd all been dressed similarly and all had been wearing black masks — it was part of their leader Hans Freidlich's plan to create a legend, the Black Mask gang, but it was also designed to create confusion and fear without actually having to hurt anyone. It was a short train, as many were in those days — just one passenger carriage and a couple of livestock and freight wagons. Jim Jackson was doing his normal thing of charming the ladies as he wandered along the carriage with a sack. He'd let them keep their wedding and engagement rings. Even though he was robbing them they seemed to love the twinkle in his eyes, and he became known as the Gentleman Train Robber.

Jim told of how he was holding open the sack for a pretty lady to drop in her purse when the man in the seat behind her started to rise, his hand already reaching for his gun.

The man was young, in his late twenties or early thirties, and smartly dressed. But there was steel rather than fear in his eyes. All of their shouting, and several gun shots fired through the roof of the train, had done nothing to scare him.

Jim said he felt his racing heart quicken further. He'd never killed a man. But he was quick. He knew he was quick enough to draw and kill this man. All he had to do was make the decision to do so.

'I'm a Texas Ranger,' the man said, as he rose. 'You need to drop that bag and raise your hands.'

Jim was about to draw when he saw

13

one of his black-masked colleagues coming up behind the Ranger. The man in the mask had a sack in his hand, one of the sacks they were using to collect money and jewellery and purses, and as the Texas Ranger rose this man dropped the sack over his head.

Jim relaxed, his gun undrawn by his side. The man squirmed and struggled and yelled. Then another of the black-masked men stepped forward, his own gun in his hand, and he placed the barrel of the gun against the struggling man's covered head, and he pulled the trigger.

Jim had told Leon how the images and sounds and smells appeared frozen in time and yet chaotically overlapped each other. The roar of the gun, the smoke, the smell of cordite and blood, the echoes of the gunshot. People screaming. The way the front of the burlap sack exploded in a red mist that coated Jim and several passengers. The Texas Ranger bounced off the back of the seat and ended up in the lap of the woman sitting next to him. The screaming grew louder. Someone shot into the roof of the train and yelled for everyone to stay still and for the men to get the hell out of there. They rushed for the door at the end of the carriage. Jim dropped the sack of money he'd already gathered. Hands reached out for him, albeit half-heartedly. There was so much confusion that these moments were blurred even as they were happening, and afterwards, after they'd made it to their horses and had ridden breathlessly away, it was no better.

Hans demanded to know who had shot the man.

Jim was covered in the man's blood, so all knew it wasn't him. Leon had been on the driver's plate. But it could have been any of the others. They argued. They examined each other's guns — but bullets had been fired into the roof of the train before and after the killing. Others had shot back towards the train as they escaped to discourage chasers. Someone said that just because Hans was the one doing the questioning didn't mean it wasn't him. Patrick Reagan said he'd been the one that had put the sack over the Ranger's head. John Allan said he thought the same man that had put the sack over the man had also shot him. William Moore said he'd been next to the killer and it was a different man to the sack man.

So it had gone on.

It had been the beginning of the end. Until then no one had ever been hurt, let alone killed, in any of the Freidlich robberies. That one killing destroyed it all.

They came for Leon Winters within a day. The others, too. Jim Jackson told how he had been packed and ready to return to his home in the east when he had opened the door and found a Texas Ranger named Sam McRae standing there pointing a gun at him.

The beginning of the end. The start of hell.

They had hanged Freidlich. Reagan and Moore had died in jail, and Leon and Jim had both suffered years of torment in the Texas Prisoner Leasing system.

The only man they couldn't account

for was John Allan. 'JA' as Jim now called him, the initials working for John Allan or Jack Anderson. It was Sam McRae, the Texas Ranger that had arrested Jim Jackson, who had later told Jim about Jack Anderson. McRae had sought out Jim Jackson to apologise for putting him away for a murder he, by then, knew Jim hadn't committed. McRae was now dead. A death that Jim Jackson subsequently avenged. These days Jim wore McRae's gun.

It was a story they had talked through numerous times.

Now Leon looked over at his sleeping friend.

It had been a hell of a journey. Maybe tomorrow, down there in Leyton, it would finally end.

3

It was morning. There was a dampness to the ground, and leaves were shining with dew. But already the early autumn sun was high enough that the first tendrils of mist were rising as the moisture evaporated. They put more wood on the fire and suspended a small pot of coffee over the flames. The smell of roasting beans soon filled the air. They toasted bread cakes for themselves and fed the horses from the oats sacks they carried — although the grass was plentiful, too.

'You think he's down there?' Rosalie asked, looking through the trees to where the town of Leyton lay out of sight on the plain below.

'He's down there,' Jim Jackson said.

'Jack Anderson or John Allan?' Rosalie said.

'They're one and the same,' Leon said.

'We *believe*,' Rosalie said. 'But we don't

know for sure.'

'We're pretty positive,' Jim said.

'Then I should go down first,' Rosalie said. 'And I should go down alone.'

Jim looked at her. 'No way.'

'Yep,' Leon said. 'No way.' 'He knows what you two look like. He doesn't know me.'

'We have to show our faces sometime,' Jim said.

'I'm not saying you don't go down ever. I'm just saying I go down first. I'll check the lay of the land.'

Leon looked at Jim. Jim shook his head.

'It makes sense,' Rosalie went on. 'You've come this far . . . For the sake of one more day. Maybe even just a few hours.'

'No.'

'I'll ride in. Buy us some fresh food. I'll look around.'

'There's no point,' Jim said. 'We have to go down there sooner or later.'

'And if there's a trap?' Rosalie asked.

'Why would there be a trap?'

'Jim Jackson and Leon Winters are both out of prison,' she said, her gaze moving between them. 'If John Allan is aware of that you think he mightn't have made some preparations?'

'How would he know?' Leon asked. But Rosalie was right. If Allan was down there and he was the one that had framed them all those years ago then he might well be on guard. Assuming someone had told him that both he and Jim were free.

'Maybe he doesn't know,' Rosalie said. 'But why risk it?'

Jim said, 'Tell me, how many people have we met on the way up here who have talked about Leyton?'

'Not many,' Rosalie said.

'But a few. And what did they say? All of them, without exception.'

'They said it wasn't a town where you wanted to put a foot wrong.'

'They said the sheriff is cruel,' Leon said. '*Desperately* cruel, was one phrase, if I remember rightly.'

'Then I'll be careful not to put a foot

wrong. Look, you know I'm right. He knows both of you.'

Jim shook his head again. 'I'm not happy about this.'

'Me, neither,' Leon said. 'It doesn't feel good.'

'But you both know I'm right,' Rosalie said again. 'Don't you?'

'You don't know what he looks like,' Jim said. But in his voice Leon could hear that Jim was reluctantly coming round to Rosalie's idea.

'He's not as tall as either of you. Black hair — though of course he may be grey, or bald by now. Brown eyes and he used to have a moustache but no beard. But that could have changed, too. Not the eyes. But the rest. He's got a scar that runs from the corner of his mouth, the left-hand side — *his* left-hand side — back towards his ear. And he's got half of his fourth finger missing on his right hand.' She took a sip of hot coffee and smiled at the men. 'That's what he looks like.'

Leon looked at Jim, smiled, and then shrugged.

'But it's not just him,' Rosalie said. 'You — *we* — want to know if there's anyone else down there waiting. It stands to reason this is where we'd turn up. And sure enough here we are. You're wanted men. There could be Texas Rangers down there waiting. You could walk right into them.'

'We left it long enough,' Jim said.

'Not through choice,' Rosalie said. 'We all took some mending.'

'Ain't that the truth,' Leon said.

'So it's agreed. I'll ride down alone.'

Jim sighed and Leon smiled. They'd both already learned you couldn't argue with Rosalie.

* * *

There was indeed something odd about Leyton, Texas. It was nothing overt, just an invisible difference to most places she'd been. The atmosphere, maybe, Rosalie thought as she rode slowly into the town. Or maybe it was the stories they'd heard from strangers on the way up here. Leyton's reputation went before it: a hard town, a cruel sheriff, not a place where you'd want to live, and definitely not a town where you'd want to do wrong. Leyton was clean and quiet and full of buildings similar to ones she had seen scores of times across the frontier. The people were the same, too. Or at least they were dressed the same. The shop-keepers and the stable-boys, the women — the wives and the daughters, the children, and over there by the Watering Hole, a couple of pretty saloon girls. Thankfully, at least a couple of the children were laughing and running around. Because, aside from those children, there was little noise in Leyton, nobody yee-hawing it up, no one snoring off last night's whiskey on the plank-walk.

She watered her horse at a trough halfway into town and then she hitched him to a rail outside a dry goods store. Somewhere someone was cooking bacon and it smelled good. She wandered along the plank-walk, casually looking in the windows. She paused outside a clothing store. There was a lady's dress on display, a blue dress in a subtle pattern with white lace on the collar and cuffs, a matching bonnet was suspended on a hook above the dress. It looked like something she might have worn in her previous life — the life that had ended a few months ago in Austin, Texas, when she had first met Jim Jackson. She had been on a train heading into Austin, dressed in a nice outfit and wearing a bonnet, with a job interview and a room at her sister's house waiting. It was supposed to be a new start, a return to a sensible life after having worked some minor frontier adventures out of her system.

Things may very well have turned out that way had Jim Jackson not sat down opposite her in the carriage and had some outlaws not attempted to rob the train.

Jim — who she discovered later had actually once been a train robber himself — had single-handedly foiled the robbery and from that moment on their lives had been entwined. Rosalie's sister, Roberta, had through her work for the State of Texas located the prison in which Jim's old friend Leon Winters was incarcerated and, armed with this information, Jim had set off to rescue Leon.

That story had ended in violence. Jim had been wounded in the process of breaking Leon out of prison. Leon had been so weak it had taken months for him to recover.

Somewhere along the way Rosalie had lost her bonnets and blue dresses and had instead found herself wearing a man's shirt and jacket, blue riding jeans, and a Colt 45 on her hip.

A sound came to her on the gentle morning breeze. She turned away from the shop window display. The noise was coming from just around the corner. It was the sound of a woman crying.

Rosalie walked towards the sound.

She turned the corner and stopped, aghast at what she saw.

There was a boy in a cage. He was no more than fifteen or sixteen. He had a shock of black hair and his face was white, his eyes red, and he was gripping the iron bars of the cage. The crying woman had her hands over his and she was imploring people to help. But nobody stopped. Few even looked.

'Please,' the woman wailed. 'Help me. He didn't *do* anything.'

Rosalie noticed a tall man, taller than even Leon, standing across the road. He had a dark hat and a very long beard and, though he was making no moves to help the woman or the boy, at least he wasn't rushing by, eyes cast downwards like most of the people.

The woman saw Rosalie.

'*Please*,' she said, more quietly than she had been a moment before. 'Help me. Help us.'

Rosalie stepped forward.

The cage was built on the outside wall of a building that she now saw was the sheriff's office. There was a door in the side of the building that had it been open would lead into the cage. The cage itself took up just half of the plank walk.

26

It wasn't big. There wasn't room for the boy to lie down and there was nothing for him to sit on. The sun was already shining down on the bars and with no shelter Rosalie could only imagine how hot it would get. It might be early autumn but the sun these last few days had felt as hot as ever during much of the day.

The boy saw Rosalie.

He shook his head, then he nodded, as if confused. His breathing was fast and she saw him trying to control his heaving chest.

'I didn't do it,' he said eventually. 'I didn't do what they said I done.'

'He didn't do it,' the woman — his mother, Rosalie presumed — echoed. 'You've got to help us.'

Another woman, scurrying by, head down, whispered 'God bless you, Martin.'

'What is this?' Rosalie said. She'd never seen anything like it in her life. She thought of the people they had passed on the ride up to Leyton, the stories they'd told. Some of those tales had seemed

fanciful at the time. But now she wasn't
so sure.

'I stole bread,' the boy called Martin
said. 'I admit that. But I didn't steal no
horse.'

'He didn't steal a horse,' his mother
said.

'Why the cage?' Rosalie said, almost
to herself. She looked round again.
More people rushed by without hardly a
glance. The tall man with the long beard
continued to watch them.

'It's to make him confess,' the woman
said. 'It gets so hot. He can't stand up
and he can't lie down.'

Rosalie now saw that the iron bars
making up the roof of the cage were just
inches above the boy's head, and he was
crouched forwards, his face up against
the vertical bars.

'I ain't confessing to something I never
did,' Martin said. 'They can send me to
prison for the bread or whip me if that's
what he wants.'

'Who's he?' Rosalie asked.

A man walking by looked at her and

shook his head. Rosalie didn't know if the shake of the head was pity or a warning.

'Him,' the woman said, nodding at the sheriff's door.

'The sheriff?'

'Yes.'

'What's his name?'

'Beelzebub, I shouldn't wonder,' the woman said.

'He whips some folks,' Martin said. 'But he don't want to whip me. He wants to . . . He wants to hang me.'

'Hang you?' Rosalie said.

'He's an evil man,' the woman said.

Behind Rosalie the sheriff's door opened. She turned, and found herself face to face with John Allan.

'At least I'm not a horse-thief,' Allan said.

He looked at her with unblinking cold brown eyes. He still had the moustache that Jim and Leon had told her about, although it was grey now. But it was the scar, white against his weather-tanned skin and running from his mouth towards his ear, that convinced Rosalie this was Allan. She wanted to glance down at his right hand, but she didn't want to give him the slightest hint that she knew who he was. So she held his gaze even though there was something in that gaze that made her tremble inside.

Behind him a deputy filled the doorway, a wide-shouldered man with a full beard and teeth the colour of coffee.

'I didn't steal any horse,' Martin said.

'We've got witnesses said you did,' John Allan said, still staring at Rosalie. 'You're new,' he said.

'Just passing through.' She still held his gaze. 'How can you keep a boy in a cage like that?'

'He can go back inside anytime he wants. He's got a cot and a jug of cool water and we'll even feed him. He just has to admit to what he did.'

'And if he didn't do it?'

John Allan stared at her and it felt just like he was reading all her innermost thoughts. She wanted to look away lest he discover Jim Jackson and Leon

Winters inside her head. But she refused to show him any weakness.

'Just passing through, you say? Then you wouldn't understand.'

'He likes to hang someone every so often,' the woman said.

'That's not true,' Allan said, turning his gaze upon Martin's mother, and to Rosalie the feeling of relief was palpable. 'I'm not afraid of hanging those that need to be hanged. This is a peaceful town. That's down to me.'

'He never did it!' the woman said.

'A lot of folks are scared to kill someone,' Allan said, looking back at Rosalie. 'Me, I take on such burdens so others can live safely. Safe in the knowledge that no one's going to sneak around in the night and steal what don't belong to then.'

'I stole bread. I admit that,' Martin said.

'You ever seen a hanging?' Allan said.

'I saw the aftermath once,' Rosalie said. 'Surely there's no need to hang him — he's only a boy.'

31

'He's old enough to steal a horse. He's old enough to hang.'

'He didn't do it!' the woman shouted.

'If you're still here in the morning,' Allan said, 'come and see him hang. Nine o'clock. I find it's a lesson that a lot of people can learn from. Anyway, if you'll excuse us.'

Then he raised his right hand to his face and saluted her and she saw that half his little finger was missing.

'You're the Devil!' the woman said to Allan as he and his deputy walked by.

He smiled at her. 'Come and find me if he confesses. He can spend his last day in the shade if that's the case.'

After the sheriff had walked away the woman turned to Rosalie. 'You've got to help us. *Please.*'

★ ★ ★

Across the street and around the corner from the cage, Rosalie paused outside the telegraph office, trying to calm her nerves.

'This is the scaredest town I ever saw.'

Rosalie jumped. She hadn't realised the tall man with the long beard was behind her.

'I saw you talking to the boy,' the man said. His voice was low and slow, steady. 'And his mother. Everyone else was too frightened.'

'They're going to hang him.'

'I heard.'

'That man . . . He really is evil. I could actually feel it.'

There were more people about now, the town was livelier, but still she could hear Martin's mother pleading and begging.

'Yes, there are men like that around.'

She looked at him. His beard was long and thick, but clean. His coat was the same. The way he looked at her, his eyes were soft but unblinking.

'Are you just passing through, too?' she said.

'Uh-huh.'

She looked down at his guns. He wore two of them.

'Maybe you could help the boy?' she said. 'His name is Martin.'

'My name is Abraham,' he said. He held out a hand.

'Rosalie.'

'Pleased to meet you, Rosalie. My advice would be to do whatever you've come to do and leave. Despite what the sheriff told you, nothing good ever came of seeing a hanging.'

'You heard?'

'He speaks loudly. He wants everyone to hear him all of the time.'

'Could you help that boy?'

Abraham smiled. His teeth were white and she thought how different he was to the sheriff and the deputy that she had been talking to just a few minutes earlier.

'No one can help Martin. The sheriff's got three deputies and they all like killing as much as he does.'

'Three?'

'Uh-huh.'

'How do you know?'

'I've been watching. Anyway, Rosalie, it's been nice talking with you. Please take my advice, and don't stick around. It's not that sort of town.'

★ ★ ★

'He's there!' she said. 'John Allan. Jack Anderson. Whatever his name is. He's there.'

Jim Jackson nodded and smiled. Rosalie knew that Jim had been sure that Anderson and Allan would turn out to be one and the same.

Leon Winters said, 'Anyone else there, though? Anyone setting a trap?'

'He's got three deputies.'

'Three?' Jim said.

'Yes. And the one I saw looked big and mean and like he would've enjoyed putting a bullet in someone.'

She took her hat off and wiped her forehead with the back of her hand. She felt so hot — hotter than the ride back up to their camp warranted. It was everything, she thought. It was the ride, it was what was happening down there in town. It was standing in front of the

35

Leabharlanna Poibli Chathair Bhaile Átha Cliath
Dublin City Public Libraries

Devil.

'How do you know he's got three if you only saw one?' Jim asked.

'I was talking to a man down there — '

'Water?' Leon interrupted, offering her a water skin.

'*He* did all the work,' Rosalie said, nodding at her horse. But she took a drink anyway. She looked over at Jim and smiled. He smiled back, but there were new lines on his forehead and his mouth barely moved from the straight. He was so close to seeing the man that had put him — and Leon — through ten years of hell that she knew he could think of little else. It was as if all his nerve endings were tuned like the highest notes of a piano.

'I didn't see any Texas Rangers,' she said. 'No soldiers. Nothing like that. But the man I was talking to down there. He was tall — taller than either of you — with a long beard and two guns. Said his name was Abraham.' She looked from Jim to Leon and back again.

'I know of no Abraham,' Jim said.

36

'Lincoln, aside.'

'Wasn't he a fellow in the Bible? Aside from Lincoln, I mean,' Leon said. He coughed gently into his hand.

'I think he was,' Jim said. 'But I don't recall him wearing two guns.'

'He was watching,' Rosalie said. 'That's the best way I can describe it. Watching.'

'Watching what?' Jim asked.

'I'm not sure. I got the impression he was watching John Allan. You know he's actually the sheriff?'

'I heard he ran the town,' Jim said. 'That's what McRae told me. It feels like a lifetime ago.'

'He's going to hang someone tomorrow,' Rosalie said. 'A boy.'

'A boy?' Leon said.

'Yes, a boy. Sixteen, seventeen. Martin. He — Martin — admits he stole some bread, but John Allan says the boy stole a horse and — '

'You *spoke* to John Allan?' Jim said.

'I was talking to the boy and his mother. Allan has him in a cage, right there on the street. It's awful. No one will help. They all walk by. They won't look. Abraham says it's the scaredest town he ever saw.'

Leon said, 'You talked to Abraham as well?'

Jim smiled at Leon.

'She's certainly does a thorough job.'

'We should help him,' she said. 'Martin, I mean. We can't let them hang a boy.'

'I don't know,' Jim said. 'We need to plan this right. Take our time.'

'Please. We don't have time. *Martin* doesn't have time. This morning you were all for riding right down there.'

She could see the tenseness in his eyes, the single-mindedness.

'What else did John Allan and Abraham say?' he asked.

She told them everything she could remember about her ride into town. After she had spoken to Abraham she had wandered around another corner and suddenly she could see the edge of town, and out there where the buildings thinned, upon a slight rise, was a graveyard. In front of the graveyard there was a gallows. A couple of fellows were hammering nails into the frame, but it looked, at least from a distance, like the frame had been there a long time. The wood was dark and weathered, and the men laughed as they worked. Aside from a few children earlier, they were the only people she had heard laugh. Maybe they were more of John Allan's deputies, she thought.

After she had told them it all they brewed coffee and sat in the shade of the trees. It was mid-afternoon. Rosalie couldn't imagine how hot it must be down in that unsheltered cage on Main Street. A month or two earlier and it was likely they wouldn't have needed to hang the boy. He would have roasted alive.

Leon said, 'What's the plan, then? Is there a plan?'

'Whatever it is, we need to save the boy,' Rosalie pleaded. 'If you'd have seen him, how scared he is. How innocent. If you saw that you'd know we have to save him.'

'The plan was always to get John Allan alone,' Jim said. 'And I guess it still is. But with three deputies, it isn't going to be easy.'

'We need a diversion,' Leon said. 'Like the one you used when you broke me out of the camp.'

'Short of setting the town alight I'm not sure I can replicate that,' Jim said.

'A hanging ought to be a pretty good diversion,' Leon said.

'What are you thinking? John Allan will surely be right there in the middle of it.'

'I'm not thinking of anything. Not in particular. But there must be *something*.'

'Something *before* the hanging,' Rosalie said.

'What do you remember about Allan?' Jim asked, looking at Leon.

'It was a long time ago. I guess I remember he liked to be in control. He didn't like it that Hans was in charge rather than him.'

'He was scared of being caught, too,'

Jim said. 'I remember he was always careful not to leave anything personal behind.'

Rosalie looked at Jim. She could sense something starting to coalesce in his mind.

'He's got his own empire now,' Jim said. 'He no doubt loves being in charge of that.'

'And,' Leon said. 'I bet he's fearful of losing it all.'

'Exactly.'

'What are you getting at?' Rosalie said.

Jim was quiet for a few moments. Then he asked, 'Was there a telegraph office in town?'

'Yes. What are you thinking of?'

Jim Jackson told them.

4

Of the many things that haunted Jim Jackson, it was the killing of a young man in the woods outside their hide-out two months ago that was the hardest to live with. He and Rosalie had successfully broken Leon out of the prison camp where he was being terribly mistreated. They'd escaped to a hide-out many miles away. But the young man in question was closing in on that hide-out when Jim snuck up on him from behind. Circumstances had meant that silence was a necessity and so Jim had cut the man's throat. From behind.

Jim had killed other men before but without exception those killings had been initiated by the other party. Jim had stood before them in fair fights. The young man in the woods had been the first one that, in Jim's mind, could have been constituted as murder.

Leon had spent weeks counselling Jim

over the killing, trying to help him to understand how it had been as fair and as justified as any of the others, that it wasn't of Jim's doing, that the circumstances had forced him into killing the man in the manner that he had.

On one level Jim knew that Leon was right and he had come to accept what he had done. But on another level, maybe in his heart rather than his brain, he still felt that he had crossed a line that he would never have imagined crossing.

Now he wondered if he wasn't going to have to step across the line once more. John Allan, the man that it appeared had framed them and set both him and Leon up for more than a decade of hell, was within reach.

But once they'd reached him, what then?

* * *

It was eight o'clock in the morning according to the clock on the wall in the telegraph office when Jim and Rosalie stepped inside. The office was neat and tidy. The walls panelled with wood, the window clean, a curtain hanging halfway up the window to maintain privacy. There was a door in the far corner — they'd already checked rear access on account of if there hadn't been any way out they would have needed to revise their plan. On a large desk below the window sat the telegraph machine — Jim wasn't sure what many of the elements did, though he was sure he could have figured it out given a few minutes. He would have loved to have simply sat down and talked to the telegraph operator about the bells and the clicker and the earpiece, the wires and all those mysterious brass instruments. Right now that was nothing but a fanciful idea. Sitting in front of the desk was that operator in a white shirt, with red braces holding up his trousers. He was balding and was wearing round-framed spectacles.

He turned in his chair.

'Good morning. How may I help you?'

Rosalie stepped forwards. They

had agreed that the request — no, the demand — would sound better coming from a woman.

'Do you think it's right that the sheriff hangs that young boy, Martin, this morning?'

The operator shifted back in his chair a few inches as if the words themselves had a physical impact.

'I'm sorry, ma'am?'

'You support the hanging?'

Jim Jackson stood in front of the door. If anyone tried to come in over the next few minutes he would say they were composing a private message — which was the truth — and could they please come back a little later.

'I . . . I'm not sure I — '

'It's a simple question,' Rosalie said. 'I was out on the street yesterday and I got the impression that most of the townsfolk are against the hanging. Maybe you're for it?'

'No. No. Not at all. It's just — '

'It's just what?'

The man leaned forwards. He reached

up and took off his glasses.

'Who did you say you were?'

'She didn't,' Jim Jackson said. The man looked over at him. Jim smiled. 'For information, we're the good guys.'

'It's just what?' Rosalie said again. Jim was impressed at how forceful she was. They had agreed on the ride down into town that she should confuse the man, bully him a little if needed.

The operator looked from Jim to Rosalie. He ran a hand over his forehead.

'What can you do?' he said. 'I mean, any of us? What can we do?'

'If you could do something, would you?' Rosalie said.

'Yes. Yes of course I would.'

'You're not scared?' Jim asked from over by the door.

'Everyone's scared.'

'Then why don't you all leave?' Jim asked.

The man looked at him. 'Oh, some folks have left. The ones that never had roots here. The ones that can afford to.'

'So you'll help us?' Rosalie said.

'What can I do?'

'If you could do something, would you?'

'Of course I would.'

'What's your name?'

'Howard.'

'Then Howard, I'll tell you exactly what you can do,' Rosalie said.

★ ★ ★

'I won't do it,' Howard said.

'Just write it out and go and hand it to him,' Jim said.

'I can't.'

'What are you scared of?' Rosalie asked.

'Look, I don't know who you are, where you come from, or what you want with Anderson —'

'We want to save that young boy,' Rosalie said.

'Well, that's as may be. But you don't live here. You don't —'

'Times getting on,' Jim said. 'If Howard here is too much of a coward —'

47

'Howard the coward,' Rosalie said, staring at the telegraph man, trying to shame him into changing his mind.

'You'd be a coward too! He'll find out sooner or later that it was made up. And when he does . . . '

A new voice piped up, 'When he finds out what?'

It was a young boy, no more than ten. He had brown hair, blue dungarees over a dirty white undershirt, and red shoes. He was smiling and standing just inside the rear door to the room.

'Billy,' Howard said. 'You shouldn't be here. Go, now. Leave.'

' 'Course I should be here. It's my job.'

Billy stepped further into the room. He smiled at Rosalie. 'My name's Billy. I run the messages for Mr Howard.'

'Hello Billy,' she said.

'Hello.' Billy turned to Jim. 'My name's Billy,' he said again. He walked forward and held out his hand. 'Pleased to meet you, sir.'

'Jim.'

They shook hands.

'Billy,' Howard said. 'You should go.'

'No messages?' Billy said, turning to look at the telegraph man.

'No, Billy. There are no messages,' Howard said.

'Actually,' Rosalie said. 'There is a message.'

'No there isn't,' Howard said.

Jim looked across at Howard, his eyes hard, and his voice level. 'The lady is right. There is a message.'

'Then give it here,' Billy said. 'I can be anywhere in town in under three minutes.'

* * *

Rosalie wrote the words in block capitals on a blank telegram. Howard was furious, telling them that it was theft, pleading for them not to put his and Billy's lives in danger. 'Our lives *after* you've gone,' he said. 'That's the thing you don't understand.'

'Oh we understand,' Jim said, after Billy had disappeared out of the door with the fake telegram in his hand. 'The thing is, this time was going to come sooner or later. And you should be thanking us from what I can gather.'

'Thanking you?'

'Your sheriff . . . Life will be a whole lot better without him. No?'

'What are you going to do?'

Jim smiled, but the smile belied his own concern — *what were they going to do?* It had been easy to come this far, driven by a white core of anger deep inside, all those years of pain, those injustices, the executions and the deaths of their old friends. But somewhere in the last few months, sometime whilst they had been recovering from injuries, when life had slowed, as the heat of summer had passed, and reason had become more . . . reasoned . . . the white hot rage had cooled. He wasn't a killer. Oh he had killed, but he was no more a killer than Rosalie or Leon were. Any man, or woman, could be a killer when they were forced into it. But when there was no longer any forcing, what then? Could he look John Allan in the eye, right here in this room, which was what they were planning, and simply shoot him?

And if not, then what?

★ ★ ★

Billy cried, 'Telegram for Sheriff Anderson! It's urgent!' He banged on the sheriff's door, his little fist not making much noise against the solid wood. He shouted again. 'Telegram for Mr Anderson!'

The cage just alongside from the door was empty. Scores of people were standing around looking at the sheriff's office. One of them, a woman, said to Billy. 'I hope to God that's someone telling the sheriff that he can't hang my Martin.' Her voice was quiet and weary. Billy looked at her. Her face was grey, with tear tracks that left darker grey lines. There were other women, and a couple of men with her. It looked to Billy like one of the men was holding Martin's mother upright. More people were arriving all of the time.

'I don't know, ma'am,' he said. 'But they told me it was urgent.'

'*They?*'

Billy looked back around. Sheriff Anderson had opened the door.

'What do you mean *they*?'

'I mean Mister Howard, sir, and the person at the other end who sent it.'

'Well give it here, boy, and don't go expecting a penny for your trouble. I'm too busy this morning to care for niceties.'

'Yes sir.'

Billy handed the sheriff the telegram and it was as if a dark magic trick had been played on the sheriff's face. As Anderson read the telegram his eyes widened and his face reddened, and then his voice burst out of his mouth louder than ever and he said, 'Darn meddlin' fools! Why can't they leave me alone?'

He screwed the telegram up in his hand and half-leapt down the steps and onto the hard, mud-packed street. He pushed Billy out of the way, sending him sprawling, and he strode across the road towards the telegraph office.

'My goodness. What did it say?' one of the men asked.

'I don't know. I can't read,' Billy said, standing up, brushing dust from his dungarees. 'But Mr Howard, he wasn't happy either.'

Then Billy ran after the sheriff.

* * *

Jim Jackson saw John Allan approaching. Allan strode across the dirt looking like a thunder storm was raging inside him. His face was red and his fists were clenched. Every step raised clouds of dark dust from the street.

Leon had been right, Jim thought. The man hated not to be in control and was terrified that all he had built up was about to be brought crashing down.

Jim was leaning against the wall of the next building along from the telegraph office. His hat was pulled down, and his head lowered. John Allan never even spared him a glance. Jim saw Billy running after the sheriff and wanted to call out to him to stay back, not to go inside. But doing so might have given the game away.

Allan smashed open the telegraph office door, letting it crash against the inside wall of the office. The door rebounded, closing itself. Jim heard him shouting at Howard, 'What in the hell is this?'

Had there been a couple of deputies with John Allan then Jim would have backed away. Rosalie was now outside, around the back of the telegraph office with the horses and with Leon. They knew what they had to do assuming all went as planned, but equally they could have all simply slipped away into the trees if the situation hadn't played out the way they had planned. Of course, if they did that, Allan would know something was up and it would make things harder — especially for Howard and Billy — but it would be better than taking on the sheriff and his deputies.

Nevertheless, Jim had figured Allan would leave at least one of his deputies guarding the boy. Probably two. So at worst he would have to deal with two men. He figured he could do that. And maybe against such odds he would find it easier to be violent. Easier to kill. He'd been leaning against the wall trying to conjure up the feelings and injustices, the pain and humiliations, the need for revenge that had driven him all these years. Seeing John Allan — their old gang-mate looking so big and healthy, so untouched by the hell that he had put the old gang through, Jim discovered that fire starting to burn within him again. He could do it, he told himself. He *could*. He could extract the revenge he had come for. He just needed to stoke that fire a little harder.

Billy was getting too close to the telegraph office. Jim stepped forwards and held up his hand to stop the boy going any further.

Jim pulled his gun from its holster.

He followed Allan into the office.

55

Billy told his friends later what had happened. He'd run up to the window and seen it all.

'The man walked in with a gun in his hand.' Billy said. 'And the sheriff, his face was still red as a beet, turned to see who it was and I'm telling you his eyes widened even more and his mouth dropped open and he shook his head, and then the man held out his gun and said something quietly and the sheriff actually smiled. He smiled and he laughed and was still shaking his head. But he put his hands up. And that was when another fellow came in from the back door and the sheriff started to twist around and this new fellow had a bag which he dropped over the sheriff's head. I mean, it was like the hood the sheriff uses when he hangs someone except these fellows were doing it to him. I mean, they must have been plumb crazy.'

★ ★ ★

56

'Remind you of anything?' Jim Jackson said, as Leon dropped the bag over John Allan's head.

'What the hell!' John Allan said, his voice still loud beneath the bag. He turned blindly, his hands first waving about wildly for balance and then reaching up to remove the bag.

Leon grabbed Allan's hands and yanked them back down.

'Oh my goodness,' Howard said from the corner of the room. 'Oh my God.'

Jim Jackson turned his gun round and cracked John Allan on the side of the head. Allan's legs gave way and he crumpled to the ground.'

★ ★ ★

'They tied him to a chair,' Billy said later. 'Lifted him up and sat him down and they tied his ankles and they tied his wrists. It took a while and I could see the sheriff starting to twist against the knots. Then the two men, they got Mr Howard's water jug and they poured it over the sheriff's head. He spluttered and he shook his head and I think he tried to say something. I just saw him shaking his head and rocking that chair.

'And then one of the men pressed his gun against the sheriff's neck.'

★　★　★

'Please,' Howard said. 'Please!'

'Shut up,' Leon said.

'I just don't want any trouble. Not in here. No shooting, please.'

The sack over Allan's head, Allan's shirt, the wooden floor below the chair were all wet. John Allan regained consciousness, twisting and turning, trying to tear himself loose from the chair. He coughed and he cursed. After he had exhausted his initial fury he became still and he said, 'You two.'

'Been expecting us?' Jim Jackson said.

There was a pause. They could hear Allan breathing heavily beneath the bag, see the material moving in and out as he inhaled and exhaled.

'Why would I be expecting you?'

'You tell us.'

Allan tried his big arms against the knots again. He sighed. 'Damn head hurts now. Why d'you do that? All we boys went through together. You could have just ridden in and said hello. I'd have even bought you a drink for old time's sake.'

'Really.'

Jim Jackson pressed the gun against Allan's neck. Allan stopped moving.

'You want to take that gun away from my neck?'

'You want to tell me why you did it?'

'Why I did what?'

'You've been talking it up,' Jim Jackson said. 'Reliable sources — the *most* reliable — informed me you'd been telling folks how you killed a Texas Ranger during a train robbery some twelve years ago. It's helped you build your reputation, that killing. Helped you build an empire run by fear.'

John Allan laughed beneath the hood.

'It's a story, my friend. A story. You

know as well as I do that I never killed anyone. I don't know who did it, but it wasn't me. It was a good story though, and sure, I appropriated it. Hasn't done me any harm.'

'Until now,' Jim said.

'You gave us up for your own skin,' Leon said.

Allan turned his head to face the new voice.

'No. You got it all wrong, fellers. Now you want to take this hood off? Move that gun, too. Let's talk it through like the old friends we are.'

Jim Jackson looked across at Leon Winters.

'Shoot him,' Leon said.

Jim was trying again to find and hold onto the fire within that had driven him for so long. But it was hard. It was too hard.

'Please!' Howard said.

Leon must have seen something in Jim's body language for he said, 'If you won't shoot him, I will.'

* ★ ★

In the main room back in the sheriff's office Emmett Maine said, 'Where in the hell is he? Townsfolk are getting restless.' The door to the lock-ups was open and they could hear the boy sobbing. Toby Moon was back there cradling a shotgun and watching the boy cry his last few earthly minutes away. They should all have been halfway to the scaffold now, dragging — maybe carrying — the boy. Instead there'd been this delay caused by a damn telegram.

Outside the crowd was getting edgy and vocal. Every once in a while, someone shouted that they were evil, that if they believed in God and justice they would let the boy go.

'Don't fret none,' Harry Dillon said. 'They ain't got an ounce of courage between them. They'll wait here until it's done. They'll cry and they'll shout and they'll spit on the ground in disgust. But secretly they're happy it ain't them. Secretly they're happy they get to sleep safely at night.'

'I'm not worried 'bout the crowd,' Maine said, looking out of the dirty window at the people outside. 'I'm wondering what's keeping Jack. He didn't look happy.'

'You want me to go and check?'

'Yeah. Can't hurt. Me and Toby have got the boy covered. Like you said, ain't no one brave enough to try anything.'

Dillon grabbed a double-barrelled Ithaca shotgun from the rack behind the sheriff's desk. Jack Anderson always recommended shotguns around town. Folks generally weren't as scared of a revolver as they ought to be, Anderson told them. But a shotgun . . . Once they've seen how much mess a shotgun can make of their faces then they get in line a whole lot quicker.

'I'll be right back,' Dillon said.

★ ★ ★

Rosalie knew she shouldn't have insisted on them rushing into something. They should have taken their time. It was just . . . How could you stand by and let them hang a young boy like that Martin? No, it had been the right thing to do to try and stop the hanging, although now, even to her, the plan felt too vague, not thought through.

She was with the horses, standing at the back of the telegraph office. The town in front of her, behind her scrub land, gently rising to the treeline. And once in those trees, well, all of Texas and beyond was there.

She knew Jim was no killer. Leon, neither. But she also knew what they had been through and why they had to do this. They had to become what they weren't, even for one second, and then they could head back into that vastness of Texas and beyond and live their lives. She did worry that after the event — after the coming killing — things might be different. No, she *knew* things would be different. Many years ago a friend who had just started studying medicine back east had explained there was always a risk when cutting out a diseased part of a body. The patient might suffer or die in the process of trying to save their life, her friend had said. But if you don't try, then the patient will surely die anyway.

Rosalie had heard the telegraph office door slam, and a moment later she had watched Leon go in through the back door with the feedbag and rope in one hand, and a drawn gun in the other.

It had felt like hours ago, although she knew it was only minutes.

And there had been no gunshot.

Yet.

★   ★   ★

Billy said to his friends later, 'Then I saw Harry Dillon coming. I didn't know what to do. I mean, I was looking in the window and these fellows had the sheriff tied up and here came Dillon and he had a shotgun in his arms and he had that look, you know, the look he gets when he kicks a dog or breaks a fellow's nose to calm him down.

'So what I did, I turned round and I said you can't go in there, Mr Dillon, sir. It's a private telegram they're writing.

'And Mr Dillon looked at me like he was going to break *my* nose. And he says, 'Is that right, son?' I said, 'That's what Mr Howard told me, sir.'

'And then he stopped, Mr Dillon did. And he slowly walked those last few yards and he peered in the window just like I had been doing.'

* * *

Harry Dillon couldn't believe it. They — two fellows — had Jack Anderson tied to a chair. He was hooded, but it was clearly Jack. And one of them had a gun pressed right up against Jack's neck.

He stepped back from the window just as the man standing next to Jack turned and looked his way.

Did he see me? Dillon wondered.

He looked at the boy, Billy. The kid raised his hands. It was almost comical.

'They made me do it,' he said. 'Made

Mr Howard, too.'

Dillon started towards the door. His urge was to kick down in the front door and burst in shooting. But then he stopped. What if that fellow had seen him? Would they be waiting? And how could he be sure he wouldn't hit Jack? The shotgun might be good for bringing a rowdy crowd to order in one of the town's saloons, but in such a small room it wouldn't distinguish friend from foe.

There had to be a better way.

Perhaps he could come in from the back? One of the fellows had been standing with his back to the rear door. He could open that door and blow that fellow's head clean off.

But what then?

What of the second fellow standing right by his boss?

No, that wouldn't work either.

What he needed was help.

'Billy,' he said.

The boy was watching him, looking scared, hands still in the air.

'Billy.'

'Yes?'

'We could hang you, you know?'

'Hang me?'

'Like we're going to hang that other boy this morning.'

'I didn't do nothing. They made me.'

'I ain't sure.'

'It's the truth. I swear.'

Dillon looked back at the telegraph building. His finger rested on the shotgun trigger. The men inside hadn't looked like they were rushing, if all they'd wanted to do was to kill Jim then they'd have done it by now. But that didn't mean things couldn't change in a heartbeat.

'Listen, maybe you can redeem yourself.'

'What's redeem?'

'Never mind. Just you run as fast as you can and you tell Emmett to get over here as fast as he can. Tell him to bring pistols.'

'And you won't hang me?'

'Just do it! Go!'

★ ★ ★

67

Jim Jackson said, 'Who was that?'

He thought he'd seen a face at the window. A movement in his peripheral vision.

'It's the boy,' Leon said.

'Billy,' John Allan said. 'His name is Billy. He's a good lad.'

'I don't want him watching,' Jim said. 'Tell him to scoot.'

'You don't want him to watch *what*?' John Allan said. 'You're Gentleman Jim. That's what they used to call you, yes? The kind one. The honourable one. You'd struggle to kill a guilty man, let alone an innocent one. And as for shooting a man tied up and hooded. Little Billy isn't going to be watching anything, is he? There's going to be nothing to watch.'

'Have you finished?' Jim said.

'I haven't done anything,' Allan said. 'Sure, I used the story to build my reputation, but I never killed anyone.'

'Listen to him!' Howard said. He had backed himself into the corner of the room, up against his telegraph table. 'You can't shoot him. It would be murder.'

'Tell the boy to make himself scarce,' Jim said to Leon.

Leon walked over and opened the door. He looked outside.

'He's gone anyway.'

★ ★ ★

Harry Dillon wandered carefully around the back of the telegraph office. He'd figured the men might have their horses there ready for a quick getaway.

He'd figured right.

Except there was also a woman there. A very pretty woman, standing with three horses, looking pale and very frightened.

He lowered the shotgun so it was pointed in the general direction of her face and he stepped into view.

'If it doesn't kill you, it'll blind you,' he said. 'You and the horses.'

She turned and her mouth opened as if to scream.

'Any sound and I'll shoot you. Now raise your hands where I can see them.'

She raised her hands and he could

69

see them shaking. He smiled. He liked it when they shook. Men or women.

'Walk towards me, slowly.'

He led her around to the front of the telegram office and here came Emmett Maine, running.

'What in the hell's going on?' Maine said, slightly out of breath. He had a pistol in his hand.

'A little bit of trouble,' Dillon said. 'But I just found us a winning card.'

* * *

'Wait!' John Allan said. 'I admit I did hear something about you two. And the other boys, too.'

'He's playing for time,' Leon said. 'Give me the word.' Leon had his own gun in his hand now.

'I can do it,' Jim said.

'Let him speak,' Howard said. '*Please*.'

'I would have done something,' John Allan said. 'But what? I mean, what could I do?'

'You were the only one didn't get sent

to hell,' Jim said. 'How do you explain that?'

Now, finally, Jim felt a little of the heat that he'd been searching for start to rise inside him. Yes, that was it. He could feel his breathing getting shorter. What he and Leon — and the others — had been through, whilst this man had been living it up, benefiting from betraying them all.

'I don't know,' Allan said. 'I guess I can't explain it.'

'Give me the word,' Leon said. 'I still get pains all over from what they did to me.'

'Just watch Howard,' Jim said. 'I figure he's looking to run.' The telegraph operator had been edging towards the rear door.

'No, no,' Howard said. 'I'm just — '

'Sit down,' Leon said.

Jim ratchetted back the hammer on the Colt.

'The fellow whose gun this was died because of what you did,' Jim said to the hooded man on the chair in front of him. 'All of your old friends died, too.'

The fire inside had caught hold now.

A few more old images and it would be raging. Then . . .

'It wasn't like that,' John Allan said. His voice was no longer so strong.

'We got beaten almost every day. The way they did it . . . What they used.' Jim shook his head even though the hooded man couldn't see the gesture. It wasn't for Allan anyway. It was for that fire. It was to fan those flames.

'That wasn't down to me.'

'It was all down to you.'

'Please.'

'It's too late for pleases. I'm sorry, but I'm not sorry, John. If you know what I mean.'

'Please!'

Jim Jackson thought back to the humiliations, the degradations, the endless agonies of his time in the prison leasing system. It all led to this moment. The fire of revenge now scorching his nerve endings.

His finger tightened on the trigger.

The sound of the gunshot was deafening in the small room, the walls capturing the sound, amplifying it, sending it bouncing from ear to ear like a wild echo. Jim Jackson felt numerous tiny stings across his shoulders and his neck and the back of his head, and suddenly the light was different in the room.

He turned, his ears ringing, and saw the upper half of the telegraph office door splintered, and then the door itself exploded inwards and there was the silhouette of a man against the morning sun, and he had a short shotgun in his hand, its barrel sawn off, and he was holding Rosalie in front of him like a shield and the barrel was pressed against her throat and he was laughing.

Even as the images and the sound registered, the rear door burst inwards and another man said, 'One move and you're both dead.'

Jim couldn't bring himself to turn away from looking at Rosalie, tears on her face, and a terrible look of loss in her eyes, but he heard Leon start to say something, he heard the sound of a gun butt on a skull, and he heard his partner crumple to the floor.

'Drop the gun,' the man holding Rosalie said.

For a moment, just a split second, Jim thought about trying to shoot the man. He might be quick enough, but any pressure on that shotgun's trigger and Rosalie would be dead.

'Drop the gun.'

Footsteps behind him. A gun pressed up against his own neck.

Jim dropped the gun.

5

'You always were a soft son-of-a-bitch,' John Allan said.

Jim Jackson looked up at him. Allan was a little out of focus from where Jim's eyes were swollen. He could taste blood, too. A tooth was loose and he couldn't help but press his tongue against it, pushing it, creating a tiny flare of pain amongst a far greater inferno. They'd beaten him, kicked him, pistol-whipped him, and finally knocked him senseless with the cut-down butt of the shotgun.

He'd come round tied to a chair in the sheriff's office.

'Used the same rope you tied me up with,' Allan had said, just after he'd thrown a cup of water into Jim's face.

Jim shook his head.

'No?' Allan said. 'What does "no" mean? You're not soft? Or that you can't believe what happened?'

Allan reached behind his head and

pulled something from the back of his collar. He looked at it for a moment and then tossed it on the floor.

'Quite pleased I had that hood on,' he said. 'It was thick enough that it was hard to breathe but at least I didn't get a headful of pellets.'

'I aimed at the roof, boss,' a wide-shouldered man with a full beard and brown teeth, standing behind Allan said. 'Didn't want to blast you.'

'I know. And I appreciate it, Emmett. You sure kept me waiting though, didn't you?'

'It's all good now though, isn't it, boss?'

Allan smiled. 'Oh yes. It's all good.'

'So, you came to kill me and you were too soft-hearted,' Allan said. 'Gentleman Jim. A dead man returning.'

Jim Jackson spat blood on the floor. His loose tooth came out, too.

'Don't be messing my office up, now,' Allan said. 'Or I'll have the girl on her hands and knees cleaning it.'

Jim looked through the open door to

the cells.

He could see Leon standing at the bars of the closest cell. In the cage beyond that was Rosalie and the young boy Martin. There were cuts and bruises on Leon's face, and even as he looked over at his friend he saw Leon start coughing and there was a spray of blood in the air.

'I'm going to hang you all, of course,' Allan said. 'One at a time. Maybe tomorrow after we hang the kid. You know, it takes a lot of arranging and you messed that up good and proper for me. Lucky for you I'm a forgiving kind. It'll be quick.'

Jim squeezed his eyes shut, trying to clear them of blood. Thoughts and images cascaded through his brain. Why didn't I just shoot him when I could? Has it all been for this? Has everything I've been through — we've been through — counted for nothing? To be hanged by the same man that betrayed us all those years ago? How could it be that I couldn't just put a bullet into him?

He could hear Martin crying in the far

77

cell. Rosalie was whispering to him, comforting him. Images of he and Rosalie whipped through his mind like tumbleweed before a storm. He remembered first meeting her on the train to Austin, a few moments before train robbers tried to rob them. She was beautiful then, as now. He loved her. And he had brought her to this. To a death in a dusty town that no one had ever heard of. Far from the city where she would have lived safe and sound to a ripe old age.

Allan's other deputies were in the office, too. The one who had come in through the back door at the telegraph office and had knocked Leon down, standing over there by Emmett, the two of them like big brothers, the same sneer, the same cold eyes, and the same stink of whiskey and sweat and cruelty rising off them in the heat of the room.

Then over to his left, another one. Not quite so wide, and a bit younger. He was cradling a shotgun in his arms like it was his baby.

'You ain't saying much,' John Allan

78

said.

'Tell me about it,' Jim said. It hurt his mouth to talk. 'It wasn't just a story was it?'

'Ah, he speaks. Tell you about it, huh? You want to go to your grave *knowing*?'

'I — we — deserve that much.'

'Well, say please, and I might.'

Jim looked up at Allan. They'd tied the knots tight. The rope was biting into his flesh. He'd tried to move his wrists, maybe work the knot loose, but to no avail. His belly was hurting. His face, his back, his legs. Everywhere. But the torture in his mind was the worst of it all.

He stared at Allan. 'Please,' he said.

John Allan smiled.

'No,' he said. 'I think I'll just let you wonder.'

From through the open door Leon said, 'You're an evil man, Allan.'

'Allan?' the one called Emmett said.

'It's just a name,' Allan said. 'I used to use it way back.'

'You did well, didn't you?' Leon said. 'Whatever you did, you did well out of it.'

Allan smiled. 'I guess I did OK. Unlike you boys. Can't imagine how you ever managed to be train robbers. Look at you now.'

'What happened?' Jim said. 'How did you do it?'

Allan walked over to his desk and opened a small box. He took out a cigar and closed the lid. Then he opened the box again and took out three more cigars. He gave one to Emmett and one to the other deputies. Each of them bit the end off their cigars. Allan scraped a Lucifer into life and then lit the cigars. He leaned against the wall and looked at Jim Jackson. Then he walked back to his desk and took out a bottle of whiskey from the bottom drawer. He pulled the cork out and took a long swig, then passed the bottle to his youngest deputy. The bottle went round the room and ended up back with Allan. He took another long drink, wiped his lips with the back of his hand and said, 'OK. I'll tell you what happened.'

The man called Abraham stood against the outside wall of the sheriff's office. His coat was open. Both his guns were visible. Anyone who knew to look for such things may have noticed that the guns rode slightly high in their holsters where Abraham had loosened them. One leg was cocked, his boot flat against the wall he leant against. He smoked a cigarette and watched the people walking by. He smiled at those that looked at him.

And he listened.

The sheriff's voice was clear through the wooden wall. He sounded excited, although there was the slightest slurring to his words as if maybe he'd partaken of a drink or two. Probably to celebrate still being alive, Abraham thought. He had gathered, from the street gossip — most of it started by a young boy — that someone had tied the sheriff to a chair over at the telegraph office and had been seconds away from shooting him dead, when the sheriff's deputies had rescued him.

Interestingly, the woman that Abraham had spoken to yesterday, appeared to have been involved in the situation. He'd liked her. But it meant nothing. Who they were didn't really matter. The situation was what it was and if their predicament could help him, so be it.

What that predicament had done was bring everyone into the same room at one time.

'They were on to us, you know. That's what happened,' the sheriff said from inside the office. 'I got a knock on the door one night and there was a couple of fellows there from the Department of Public Protection, or so they said. I wasn't sure. I'd never heard of such a department. But there they were. There were a couple more of them outside. I saw them. The one who had knocked on my door told me that they'd come to arrest me and he painted a pretty grim picture of what lay ahead.'

Abraham heard someone else interject at that point but he couldn't make out the words.

'They took me away and I thought that was it. Locked me in a room overnight. But in the morning they offered me a deal.'

'You double-crossed us,' someone else said.

'No. They said if I were to do something real simple for them, just one thing, they would make all of the trouble — that future in hell-holes like you ended up in — go away. I thought he meant for all of us.'

'Like hell you did.'

There was a pause then. Maybe, Abraham thought, the sheriff was shrugging. Yes, from what he'd seen of the sheriff that's what he'd be doing.

'All I had to do was kill a man on a particular train,' the sheriff went on. 'They basically set up that robbery. It wasn't easy. I honestly didn't want to give you guys up — '

'So you *did* betray us.'

'It was falling apart anyway. We were on borrowed time and they had us anyway. They knew who we were and where

83

we lived, and if I'd have said no you'd have all been arrested by morning anyway.'

'And to think I hesitated from pulling the trigger just a few minutes ago.'

'Like I said, you always were soft. Anyway that's it. It couldn't have worked out better, the way one of you dropped a sack over his head. I knew I had to kill the fellow, but I didn't know how until that moment. That's it. That's all I know. After that you went your way and I went mine.'

'We went to Hell and you came here and lived like a king.'

'The wind blows different ways for different folks. It's the way it is. Emmett, untie him. Let's put him back in the cell.'

Abraham heard the jangle of keys. He counted to ten.

Then he pushed himself away from the wall, drew his guns, and kicked open the door.

★ ★ ★

Jim Jackson was standing in the doorway between the room in which the cages were situated and the sheriff's office. John Allan was in the cage room with the keys to one of the cages in his right hand and a Colt 45 in the other. He was unlocking the cage in which Leon stood, blood specks on Leon's lips from his coughing, his hands gripping the bars.

Emmett — Jim didn't know his surname — was standing in the sheriff's office loosely holding a shotgun, which pointed in the vague direction of Jim Jackson's spine. The other two deputies still lounged against the wall in the office, enjoying their cigars, filling the room with a warm rich smell, which at least temporarily masked the stink of sweat and body heat.

All of the lawmen looked relaxed and carefree, almost jolly. The sheriff even seemed a little drunk. Drunk on life, Jim thought. When you come as close to death as Allan had, then it doesn't take much liquor to make you happy. Just being alive is enough.

And if, in the process, you capture the man who was going to kill you. Well, that's just like drinking another bottle of good whiskey, isn't it?

Jim swallowed, tasted blood, and wondered if he'd ever be drunk on life again. He looked into the first cage and saw Leon standing there, still gaunt. He worried about Leon's cough. Leon always tried to hide it but Jim had noticed. Rosalie, too. A cough like that, when you're spitting blood, is a killer. And Rosalie, in the next cell along, her arm around the boy who was to hang the next day. How had he allowed this to happen to sweet beautiful Rosalie?

Allan was just slipping the key into the door lock, saying something to Leon about moving to the back of the cage if he knew what was good for him, when Jim heard something crash against the door, and then he heard the secondary smash as the door itself hit the inside wall.

He turned.

The man with the long beard was

quick. As quick as Jim had ever seen.

The gun in his right hand blazed twice, two flashes of fire, two blasts so close together that they may have been one.

Both deputies against the far wall fell, not even enough time for recognition or awareness to register in their eyes.

Emmett was turning now, the shotgun swinging towards the bearded man.

But the gun in the man's left hand blazed, too, and Emmett was lifted off his feet and thrown against a chair. Emmett's finger squeezed the shotgun trigger as he fell and the blast ripped into the office ceiling.

The realisation struck Jim that the bearded man couldn't see John Allan. And that even if the angles of the wall had allowed that visibility then he, Jim, was in the doorway between the two men.

John Allan was still holding the keys, but now he was turning, straightening up.

'Catch.'

The bearded man didn't wait for a response. He gently lobbed one of his guns towards Jim Jackson. Jim would never know if was luck or judgement — the latter he suspected afterwards, on account of how efficient the bearded man had been with everything else — but the gun landed perfectly in Jim's hand.

He'd been beaten. He'd been tied up. The knots overly tight. The blood was only just coming back into his hands. The nerve endings were tingling. His fingers felt as big as sausages.

But instinct took over.

John Allan was raising his own gun, when Jim Jackson shot him. Once. Twice. Three times. The bullets smashing Allan into the far wall, leaving a smear of blood where he'd slid down the grey paint.

He was dead without ever seeing, or knowing of, the bearded man who had come to kill him.

6

Years later it would become known as the Leyton Massacre. It wasn't a story that was ever documented as the towns-folk didn't want anyone hunted down or prosecuted. Those townsfolk were free of the tyrant that had ruled their lives for years. The fear lifted from Leyton like morning mist burned off the creek by a late summer sun. The story became a whispered and joyous hand-me-down, shared by the generations, but always a town secret. And part of the tale was of the celebrations that day and night. Celebrations that became a great fiesta. Pianos and fiddles were played with a freedom and a spirit that few in the town could recall. The tall bearded man — Abraham — was a hero, albeit a reluctant one. He drank just a little that day, and was happy to hold hands and dance in the street once or twice. Jim Jackson, Leon Winters, and Rosalie

Robertson were feted, too. They danced and drank, too, and even Howard from the telegraph office, albeit begrudgingly, forgave them the way they had forced him into their plot. Young Billy's stories grew wilder every time he retold them, but there was no denying he had been there, right in the midst of it. Martin and his mother couldn't find the words to thank Rosalie, although they tried over and over, and in the end they simply offered their home as a place to stay whenever Rosalie or her men, as Martin put it, needed one.

It was on the floor in that house that Jim Jackson woke the morning after the celebrations, with a head that hurt more from the beating that John Allan had given him and the scores of tiny pellet wounds from the shotgun blast than from the whiskey he had enjoyed.

He rose, pulled on his boots, and stepped outside.

The morning was fresh, crisp and still. On the plank-walk across the street a couple of young men were still sleeping off the celebrations. A dog wandered along the centre of the street, sniffing the ground, its tail wagging as if it, too, had found some new freedom. A vee of geese flew south-east, and a gentle breeze lifted a whisper of dust from the boards on which Jim Jackson stood.

He'd killed a man again. But this time it didn't bother him as other killings had done. In fact he had enjoyed it in a way. He — *they* — had been facing death, and to shoot a man whose intent was your own killing felt right. Even, in some ways, honourable. He had done the right thing by Rosalie and Leon. For a man to save his friends that way felt good. To go from feeling like you were responsible for their forthcoming execution to the point where you had rescued them, there was no better feeling.

Yet that good feeling worried him.

Was he starting to enjoy it? Was he, with every man he killed, becoming immune to it?

But it wasn't even those questions that were bothering him most this morning.

It was something more. He had done what he had set out to do. The last few months had been leading to this. This killing of the man who had betrayed them and consigned them to so many years of misery.

Yet . . .

What was it Allan had said?

They said if I were to do something real simple for them they would make all of the trouble go away. All I had to do was kill a man on a particular train. They basically set up that robbery.

They.

Who were *they*?

There had been someone behind what Allan had done. Sure, it had been down to Allan, but on another level — a bigger level — it was down to someone else.

He had tried to talk to the one called Abraham about it yesterday. But Abraham had been elusive. Oh he had talked. He had commended Jim Jackson on his gun-work — and his catching ability — and he had admired the Colt that Jim Jackson had strapped back on after Allan had been killed and they had retrieved their own weapons from the sheriff's drawer. Abraham had been charming to them all — especially Rosalie — and he had enjoyed a few drinks at the celebrations, but any direct question about who he was, and why he had come to Leyton, had been deflected with a smile and a shrug.

Well, that had been yesterday. Emotions, especially relief, had been flooding through everyone, the whole town, but especially Jim. Today, with a bit more sense and time in the air, Jim Jackson would try again. Someone else had forced John Allan to kill a man on a train, and that someone else had been responsible for Jim and Leon's hell, and the death of their other friends — Hans Freidlich, Patrick Reagan and Bill Moore. Hans, who had been their leader, had been hanged after the murder on the train that John Allan had committed. Pat had died in Huntsville of pneumonia, and Bill had been shot when, unable to bear the hell no longer, he had run from a chain gang. All of them gone. It could all be laid at John Allan's door, but who had put it there?

The fact that Abraham had arrived to kill John Allan had to be connected. No question. Jim didn't know where Abraham had spent the night. But this morning he would find him, and he wouldn't let Abraham leave until he knew what Abraham knew.

★ ★ ★

'He's gone,' Jim said.

They were sitting in Rose's Café, just down from the Watering Hole, and diagonally across the road from the sheriff's — currently empty — office. Leon and he were eating boiled ham, beans, and eggs and drinking coffee, and Rosalie had toasted bread with cheese and sausage on the side. They had mugs of very good coffee, and it was all free. Rose had insisted on feeding them free of charge for as long as they were in town. As they ate many people came up and thanked them, shook their hands, and offered such gratitude that it started to become embarrassing.

'He's gone?' Leon said.

'Who?' Rosalie asked.

'Abraham. I checked at the Livery this morning. He left in the early hours.'

'I liked him,' Rosalie said.

'He saved our lives,' Leon said. 'Does it matter he's gone?'

'It's not over,' Jim said. 'You heard what Allan said.'

'Someone made him do it.'

'Yep.'

'What are we going to do?'

Jim shrugged. 'What can we do?'

'Maybe it's time to let it go,' Rosalie said, lifting her coffee mug. 'John Allan got what was coming to him. You avenged your friends. Maybe it's time to go home?'

'Home?'

'Home,' she repeated.

'Where is home?' Jim said. He looked at Leon. 'Where's your home, Leon?'

Leon shrugged. 'No idea. You?'

'The same.'

They both looked at Rosalie.

She smiled. 'I don't know either. Not these days.'

'So we can't go home on account of we have no home. What do we do then?'

'More bacon?' Leon said.

'More bacon,' Jim agreed. But the unfinished business still bothered him.

★ ★ ★

Howard sat at his desk with a book open in front of him.

When he heard the squeal from his damaged door he turned, and Rosalie saw that he had a monocle gripped in one eye and was holding a small screwdriver in his right hand.

Rosalie held up her hands as if offering a peace gesture.

'I'm not going to force you to do anything,' she said. 'Not today.'

Howard managed a small, almost straight, closed-lipped smile.

'I've come to say thank you. And to

apologise,' Rosalie said.

Howard put the screwdriver down, then reached up and took the monocle from his eye.

'I pulled the wires from the key,' he said, by way of explanation. 'I don't know when, it must have been yesterday during all that . . . excitement.'

'I'm sorry we had to do what we did.'

'I'm sorry I acted the way I did. I was scared. I'm no hero. I . . . If you'd have lived here then . . . Well you won't understand. You can't understand.'

'I think I do. The celebrations last night. It was quite revealing.'

'It's still scary,' Howard said. 'I mean it's a vacuum now. Do you know what I mean? No one's in charge.'

'Just enjoy it, Howard. I'm sure there are men in town who can step into that vacuum.'

'Maybe your friend? Friends, I mean. Both of them.'

'It's time for us to move on.'

'You came to kill him? Nothing more? Now you're going?'

97

'It's a long story. A very long one. Anyway, I just wanted to apologise before we left. I don't normally behave that way. It was all an act.'

She stepped closer and held out her hand.

'No hard feelings?'

'No hard feelings.'

He shook her hand, and this time his smile was a tiny bit wider. She saw that the book on his desk was open to a wiring diagram.

'Jim would love to talk to you about that,' she said. 'He loves the mechanical.'

'It's electrical.'

'I'm sure he'd be interested in that, too. Anyway, I hope you get it fixed before someone wants to send a message.'

'Oh I already have a spare. I set it up this morning when Abraham came in.'

'Abraham?'

'Yes.'

'I thought he left in the early hours?'

'I was still awake. People were still partying. The noise . . . '

'And he sent a message?'

'I shouldn't have said anything.'

'What did he send? Who did he send it to?'

Howard shook his head. 'I couldn't possibly say. It's private. It always is. It's all we have — that absolute privacy. If people thought we were sharing their messages . . .'

'Howard. It's important.'

'I'm sorry. I can't.'

'After all we've done?'

'That was different.'

'I know it was different! That was life and death. We saved a young boy from being hanged and we freed an entire town. All I'm asking —'

He shook his head. His face was reddening slightly. 'Please don't ask.'

'What do you think they'll say?' She waved her hand in the general direction of the door, and by implication, the town beyond it. 'Everyone out there is giving us whatever we want. Even when we don't want it. We can't pay for a drink, a meal, a bath, a haircut. Someone even offered to look at my teeth. Anything we want is ours this morning. You think they'd take kindly to you refusing to give me one little thing?'

'They'd understand.'

'Howard. *Please.*'

He looked down at the screwdriver, at the book. He sighed.

'It's connected, isn't it? Abraham, I mean.'

'It might be.'

He sighed.

'I need to pop out the back for a moment.' He paused. Then he said, 'Please don't go through the drawers looking for the records of what I've sent.'

'Thank you, Howard.'

'For what? I haven't done anything.'

Then, without looking at her, he stood up and walked out of the back door.

★ ★ ★

She put the slip of paper down on the table in front of Jim and Leon. They were alone at the big table in Martin and his mother's kitchen. Something was simmering in a large black pot on the stove in the corner and the room smelled of ham and coffee and herbs.

The note was addressed to *Beecher and Smith, Austin, Texas.*

'That's your writing,' Jim said. He'd never forget her writing. A note once that gave him the address of the prison camp where Leon was being held, and a short while later another letter to say that she was in the town adjacent to that prison camp when he'd thought he'd never see her again. Both moments were seared into his memory like a brand on a calf.

'I copied it out.'

Leon picked up the note.

'Who are Beecher and Smith?'

'No idea,' Jim said.

'Austin,' Leon said.

Jim felt his insides churn. He'd escaped the capital by the skin of his teeth not so long ago. People had died — and although he wasn't to blame, he knew the authorities there held him accountable. They would love to get their hands on him and Leon again. The thought made him go cold.

'Austin,' he repeated. His throat dry. He reached across the table for the jug of water.

'*Job Done. JA killed.*' Leon read.

Rosalie had even copied out the header: *Western Union. Four words.*

'Beecher and Smith,' Jim said. 'Austin.' His hand shook a little as he poured water from the jug into his cup. Every time he thought he had escaped Texas, or some part of Texas, it seemed something wanted to drag him back.

7

There was something a little more uncontrolled, wilder, and even violent about Washington Smith's lovemaking. No, *violence*, wasn't the right word, Evelyn decided. It was crazy, that's what it was. It was as if a great weight had been lifted from his mind and the relief had set him free, and he'd grabbed that freedom with both hands, and both legs, and . . . well something else as well. And here they were in this small but beautiful Austin hotel where the bed sheets smelled of wild flowers and where there was indoor plumbing on the ground floor. They'd enjoyed a meal and too much wine. His wife thought he was out west somewhere at one of his timber places, and he'd been like a wild stallion suddenly let out of a corral in rutting season.

She liked Washington. She really did. He was handsome in a greying, ageing way. Although these last few months he'd been far too tense, had too many new lines mapped onto his forehead. He was powerful, of course. Not just the money — although there was that — but the way he controlled men, controlled his empire. Even the way he controlled Charles Beecher, his supposed equal. She enjoyed their evenings and nights together. Oh it was wrong, she knew that. Just as she knew there was no future in it. He talked about leaving Martha but she knew — and Washington knew — that it was just talk. But so be it. She was single, even if he wasn't. She hadn't set out to be a mistress — it had simply happened. She had fallen a little in love, just the way a thousand other people did every day, especially when they worked so closely. At some point she'd have to figure out what to do about the situation. She knew that she was trapped to a certain extent, imprisoned by a job and an affair and if she didn't break loose she would never find her own true freedom and happiness in life.

But that was all for another day. Right

now it was so nice to see and feel the relief coursing through his body, even if it had made him a little wilder and crazier than normal.

Afterwards, Washington lay back against the pillow. He rested a glass of whiskey on his bare chest, the glass nestling amongst his curling grey chest hairs.

'He's dead,' Washington said.

'Who?' She propped herself on an elbow and looked at him. For a moment she thought he meant Charles Beecher. Sometimes she got the impression that Washington felt Charles was holding him back. There was a tiny flare of fear at the back of her neck. Was he capable of that?

'Just someone from long time ago.'

He took a sip of whiskey, put the glass on the table by the bedside, and turned to look at her.

'A loose end,' he said, and smiled. He lifted the whiskey glass, took a sip, and then placed the glass on the small table beside the bed. 'I feel very good. Make love to me, Evelyn.'

Roberta Robertson sat in her favourite armchair reading The Adventures of Huckleberry Finn. Everyone was reading it. She'd bought a copy the weekend before in Gammel's bookstore. The book was heavy, the hard cover green and embossed gold, and the words inside were full of adventure, fun, and wonderful characters. Each night, after she'd eaten and cleared up, Roberta sat in her chair, an oil lamp at her shoulder, and fell deliciously into Huck's world. A world she longed to partake in, but knew she never would. That was the beauty of books — you could partake of the adventure whilst sitting in a comfortable chair, with a glass of sherry on the table, and a door between you and the rest of the world.

At one point she found her mind wandering. It wasn't that the words weren't gripping — they most certainly were — but they had created resonances, memories, and ideas in her mind. She found herself thinking of her sister Rosalie. Rosalie who would happily have jumped on board that raft with Huck Finn and ridden the river to wherever it took them.

Rosalie had travelled through the frontier territories just a few months ago, out where the west was still wild. Rosalie had embraced the adventure but Roberta had eventually managed to persuade her sister to come to Austin and get a proper job. She'd rather hoped her sister would find a man like she'd done. Her own *beau*, Andrew, was a lawyer. A handsome lawyer. Roberta was quite excited about the future, although she was taking things slowly. She'd worked so hard for this little house and her independence that she was reluctant to let things change too rapidly. Nevertheless, she had a wonderful feeling about the future and it would be nice to have her sister close by, and with Rosalie's looks and her lust for life she'd be sure to find an Andrew of her own very easily.

Actually, Roberta thought, the truth

was Rosalie had already found a man. But that man was a killer and a train robber, albeit one that appeared to have swapped sides. He'd foiled a train robbery the very day that Rosalie was riding the train into Austin. Within a day Rosalie had gone out walking with him. But not before Rosalie had persuaded her — Roberta — to use her position at work to find information about a series of men that, it turned out, were, or had been, in prison throughout Texas. Most of those men were dead. But one — Leon Winters, Roberta remembered the name — was still alive. And sure enough, this handsome ex-train robber had disappeared the very next night, leaving Rosalie high, dry and abandoned. That should have been the end of it. But oh no, just like Huck Finn was swept from one adventure to another, that same night Rosalie came home weeping. Two of her fingers had been broken. Roberta had never quite worked out the whole story, but she knew it had all revolved around the train robber. And then a few days later, Rosalie, and her broken fingers, had disappeared.

A life of danger and adventure. It was foolhardy and it was something of which Roberta disapproved, whilst, deep inside she was quietly jealous.

She sighed, took a sip of sherry, and focused on Twain's words again.

Half an hour later someone knocked on her door.

Roberta slipped a thin strip of brown leather into the book to mark her place. She put the book onto the table next to her empty sherry glass. She went across the room and opened her door.

'Hello sister,' Rosalie said.

* * *

Roberta said again, 'I can't believe it. I mean — '

'You can't believe it,' Rosalie added.

'I was just thinking of you. *Really*. It's almost . . . It's like magic.'

They were sitting in Roberta's small front room. The Mark Twain book lay forgotten on the table, although Roberta had picked up and refilled the sherry glass. She'd poured Rosalie one too, and was now sitting on the two-seater next to her sister.

'Tell me *everything*. How's your hand? Let me see. I never thought I'd see you again. What really happened? Where did you go? Tell me it all!'

'I've never heard you talk so much, sis',' Rosalie said.

'Oh, I'm sorry.'

'No, don't be.'

'It's just . . . I'm so excited. I really didn't think I'd see you again. I was so sad. I was desperately sad. You just . . . left.'

'I couldn't tell anyone where I was.'

'But where were you? Why couldn't you tell?'

'It's a long story.'

'It's Friday, Rosie. There's no work tomorrow. We've got all night. Are you hungry?'

'I'm — '

'You look hungry. You look thin. Those

110

clothes. They look like men's clothes.'
Roberta shook her head disapprovingly.

'That's more like the Roberta I know,'
Rosalie said.

'Oh, I'm sorry.'

'I'm joking.'

'Oh. But you do look like . . . You *are*
dressed like a man.'

Rosalie smiled. She sipped sherry from
the tiny cut glass. She looked around
the room. The curtains were heavy and
beautiful, as were the cushions. There
were paintings on the wall, books on a
shelf. A plaster cornice ran around the
room between wall and ceiling, and halfway up was a dado rail. She'd forgotten
how beautiful Roberta had made her
small house. Outside, in the street, there
had been streetcars — like stagecoaches
but long and slow and much more comfortable looking. And hanging alongside
and across the roads were electric lights.
Now *that* was magic.

The sherry was sweet and warm.

It was safe, civilized living. It was
living like living was meant to be for a

young professional woman in this modern world.

It was, Roberta had told her last time, what Rosalie could have if she got a job and settled down.

Rosalie thought of Jim and Leon, camped several miles out of Austin, hidden in the woods, no walls between them and the rest of the world, no ceiling between them and the stars.

'These clothes are practical,' Rosalie said. 'Out there.'

'*Out there*,' Roberta said. 'Is he still out there? The train robber man.'

Rosalie smiled.

'Let me get you something to eat,' Roberta said. 'And you can tell me all about it.'

★ ★ ★

The electric lights outside had long gone off by the time Rosalie had told her sister almost everything. Roberta had been full of questions throughout the story, but now she was quiet.

Rosalie took the quietness for disapproval, something her sister had always been good at.

'I suppose you had to be there,' she said.

'He's a wanted man,' Roberta said. 'They both are.'

'In the eyes of the law, yes. But as I said, if you'd have been there.'

Roberta shook her head.

'I'm not judging.'

'What then?'

'I thought I'd lost you once before. That you'd gone forever. You'll no doubt be going again soon.'

'I'm sure one day we'll . . .'

'What?'

'Settle down.'

'You think?'

'Yes.'

'Why did you come back? I mean, why now?'

'You're my sister.'

'You want something, don't you? Let me guess: you want to know about Beecher and Smith.'

'Yes and yes. But you're my sister. I will always come and see you.'

'Your old bed is still made up. Let's talk more in the morning.'

⋆ ⋆ ⋆

Leon stood with his forearm against a tree, his forehead on his arm, and he rested from the coughing whilst half spitting, half dribbling blood onto the ground. It was getting worse, and he could no longer hide it from Jim.

'We need to get you to a doctor,' Jim said.

They'd been camped for two days and two nights in the same quiet spot. They were off the beaten track, in a dense copse of trees that grew hard up against a sheer rock face, many miles to the west of Austin. A stream ran through the trees, and there was grass on the ground where the sunlight forced its way through the canopy, and the rock face protected them from the wind and from anyone approaching from behind.

'There'll be time for that once this is done,' Leon said.

'I'm told the doctors in Austin are as good as any in the world.'

'Who told you that?'

'Well, I imagine they are. You should see it — Austin. It's like something out of the future.'

'You know that neither of us can show our faces in Austin. Well, especially you.'

'We may have to yet.'

'So be it. But I'm OK. Truly. A few nights with good whiskey and a warm blanket and I'll be fine.'

Jim said nothing. He knew the signs of consumption. A dry climate was what was needed. That and rest. But there must be something a good doctor could do as well. The way Leon was sounding, by the time *this* was over — whatever this was — and he came to take his rest it might be too late. Jim stood up, still aching from the beating that John Allan had given him in Leyton, and put another couple of dry broken branches on their low fire. The sky was darkening. It was surprising how quickly the air chilled once the moon was up. He thought of his own warm blanket. It wasn't nearly so warm without Rosalie there.

'You think she's OK?' Leon asked.

'She's fine,' Jim said, wondering if he'd mentioned Rosalie's name aloud.

'You any ideas on Beecher and Smith?'

'None at all.'

'I've been thinking on it.'

'Beecher and Smith?'

Leon came away from the tree and sat by the fire.

'Yes, but also on that fellow that John Allan killed on the train. Why would someone — presumably this Beecher and Smith — want a Texas Ranger dead?'

'Go on.'

Leon coughed into his hand. Through new habit he looked at his hand and then wiped the blood on his trousers.

'And why would they want it to look like an accident? Well, not an accident, but like it was the result of a train robbery?'

'Uh-huh.'

'I think the Ranger could be the key.'

'He knew something?'

'Or he was close to knowing something,' Leon said.

'It was over ten years ago,' Jim said.

'Yep.'

'And we can't exactly walk up to a Ranger and ask, even if we knew where to find one.'

'Maybe we could.'

'You're crazy, Leon.'

'You told me once about that fellow McRae. The one whose gun you carry. He knew something.'

'Sam McRae. And he's dead, too.'

'He knew you were innocent — and, by implication, me too. And if he knew something then maybe someone else does, too?'

'I doubt it. I suspect it ended with McRae.' But, Jim thought, maybe Leon was right. Maybe Leon was onto something here.

'McRae was killed by someone else. You told me it was unrelated — a black-mail racket, you said.'

'Yes.'

'And you avenged his death?'

'Uh-huh.'

'So firstly I don't think the Rangers would look unkindly upon you. And secondly, I'm not sure anyone has put all this information together. We can't. Not quite.'

'You want me to walk up to a Ranger and ask?'

'I don't know. Like I said, I'm just thinking on it.'

'Let's see what Rosalie comes back with about Beecher and Smith. She'll be here in the morning. Maybe noon. It's a fair way.'

★ ★ ★

Rosalie told the men: 'They run a lumber yard.'

'A lumber yard?' Leon said.

'Yes. Just outside of the city. A place called Georgetown. Roberta said their operation is huge, and the two of them — Mr Beecher and Mr

Smith — are both bigwigs on the social scene. They're rich and they're influential. That's *very* rich and *very* influential.'

Jim Jackson rested a metal pot on the flat stones that he'd placed alongside the fire when they'd first set up camp. The stones were burned black now and were retaining heat well. He edged the pot so half of it was hanging over the flames. It would take a while to boil, but then anything good was worth waiting for.

Leon coughed into his cupped hands, and said, 'Why would lumber men send Abraham to kill John Allan?' Even as he said the words he raised a finger as if to say, *actually, I think I might know.*

Jim Jackson smiled. He was on the same line of thinking.

'They wanted to kill John Allan so as he wouldn't talk to us,' Leon said. 'It only happened after you were released and once you'd broken me out of that camp.'

'Yep,' Jim said. 'Until we were free they had no worries.'

'John Allan was the only connection

119

between us and them.'

'Yep.'

'And they'd be interested in us because of . . .' Leon let the word hanging so that Jim could complete the sentence.

'Lumber,' Jim said.

Rosalie squinted in puzzlement. Now she held up a finger. "Hold that thought," she said. She opened her saddlebag and pulled out bread and dry beef, cheeses, and a bottle of wine. The men looked at the food, then at one another. They both smiled. It was hungry work sitting in a camp waiting. Especially when your food was running low.

Rosalie spread a cloth on the floor and placed the food on it.

Once they were tucking into the fresh food Rosalie asked: 'Lumber? What's the connection?'

'Leon spent ten years cutting down trees,' Jim said. 'Me, too.'

'Guess how much we got paid?' Leon said.

'I'd guess nothing, if you were prisoners.'

'You'd guess right,' Leon said.

'So you think the trees you cut down for nothing might have ended up in Beecher and Smith's yard?'

'Why not?' Leon said. 'Cheap wood. Very cheap wood for very rich men.'

'But why would they want to kill someone over that?'

'I don't know,' Leon said. He coughed and pulled a pained face.

Rosalie looked at him. There was concern in her eyes. 'I asked my sister something else, too. I asked her if she knew a good doctor in the city.'

8

Leon looked around in awe. Jim had been right — Austin was like something out of the future. It had been so long since he'd been in a city. In the years he'd been away, both on the trail and in the prison camp, it appeared that buildings had both multiplied and grown taller. There were so many streets it surely must be impossible to memorise where you were, or indeed where anyone else was. There were parks and fences, great mansions, not out on the plains, but right here in the middle of a town. Churches and hotels that stretched upwards like they were trying to touch the clouds. Up on a hill in the centre of Austin there was construction taking place of a great building that did indeed touch the clouds, albeit the autumn mist was low this morning. And the people, so many people. Walking, standing, sitting on benches, riding horses and ponies, being carried in buggies and in long open-topped coaches. There were crowds of people on the plank-walks — except they weren't plank-walks, they were stone walkways — bustling in and out of doorways, buying and carrying, talking and laughing, debating, haggling, arguing. Young girls, old women, business men, children, folks wearing spectacles and carrying books, men wearing suits. There were a few trail hands too, but only a few.

'I didn't think anyone would recognize me,' he said.

'They won't,' Rosalie assured him.

'But they'll know I'm different. Look at them all. I stick out like a hornet stung me on the nose. They're staring at me.'

'It doesn't mean they recognize you. Did you ever have your photograph taken?'

'Photograph? Actually yes. A long time ago when I was arrested. There was a fellow that took my photograph. I remember thinking that it was strange. He never took anyone else's, none of the

123

other prisoners I was with. Just mine.'

'I doubt anyone here is carrying around that picture.'

'I was different then,' Leon said. 'Younger. I hadn't been through . . . I hadn't been through anything.'

'Then no one will recognize you.'

'I still think this is a bad idea.'

But even as he spoke Leon felt the tickle in his chest that he knew in a few seconds would turn to a scratch, and then into a lung-squeezing pain. He coughed into his hand. There was more blood than there had been recently and he made to lean over and spit on the ground. But he noticed a pretty girl just to his left looking at him as if he was from China or somewhere. She was well-dressed and her hair was piled high and it glistened cleanly in the sun. Just by being himself he was attracting too much attention. He swallowed the blood instead, grimacing at the coppery taste and the thick consistency.

'Are you all right?' Rosalie asked.

'I'm fine. I keep telling you all.'

'You're not fine. I saw you last night spitting out blood. I heard you coughing. And I heard you moan a few times, too. We'll get something for you. My sister will take us to the doctor.'

'And he'll have a magic cure.'

'It won't be magic. But it'll be something. We don't want to lose you, Leon.'

★ ★ ★

Jim Jackson had elected not to ride into the city with Rosalie and Leon. 'It wasn't that long ago that I was in Austin,' he said. 'I really don't want to show my face there again. Not so soon.' Instead, he'd said, he'd ride out and see how the land lay around Beecher and Smith's yard. 'I don't know what I'm looking for,' he said. 'Maybe just an idea. Maybe something I'll know when I see it.' It was how he'd worked back in Prairie City, where Leon had been held in the prison leasing camp. He'd gone up there and he'd ridden around, waiting and searching for an idea to form, a way to break Leon out.

And lo and behold an idea did form, and it worked, too.

There'd be no harm in taking a casual look at Beecher and Smith's operation.

Jim found the railroad tracks before he found the trail. He pulled his horse to a halt and watched a lumber train smoking slowly southwards. The locomotive, a 2-8-0, pulled dozens of flatbed wagons, each piled high with raw timber. The smell of burning coal from the smokestack filled the air and the wheels rattled over the rails. It felt like an age before the brakeman's wagon with the red light on the back disappeared from sight.

'Lot of timber,' Jim said to his horse.

He squeezed his heels against her flanks and together they followed the tracks, until a mile or so later he picked up a hard-packed, wheel-rutted trail that crossed the rails, and then ran alongside them towards a distant cluster of buildings. It was a cluster that grew and grew as he approached, as did the fire and smoke, the noise of machinery and the smell of more burning coal.

He arrived at a set of huge metal gates. The gates were open, not that they were designed for anything other than show. They weren't connected to anything. One could have ridden around them just as easily as through them. The railroad tracks entered the site just along and to the right of the gates. Looking further out, it did appear that a line of barbed-wire marked some of the perimeter of the site.

He rode around that perimeter, looking in at the vast workings, the steam engines, and the long platform from which cranes were unloading the logs the train had just brought in. The logs were floated down further into the site on water courses built behind and parallel to the platform. There was a cookhouse and several bunkhouses, a building that looked like a saloon, coal heaps and numerous fires, water tanks, and stables. As he rode leisurely around the perimeter, Jim spied a blacksmith. There was a huge office building made of bricks. He circled it all and on the far side rode up onto higher ground, where he sat looking down on the empire and wondered if his and Leon's sweat and blood had paid for any of it.

* * *

Washington was drinking. He'd been drinking since midday. He was standing by his office window looking out, a glass in his hand. A few minutes earlier he'd been looking at the map on the wall with the little blue pins that showed where their lumber camps were. There'd been a glass in his hand then, too.

'Just when you think you've got a handle on it all,' Smith said. 'Just when you damn well think everything is finally good again.' He lifted the glass to his lips, poured all of the whiskey into his mouth, and threw his head back violently as if swallowing a nasty potion.

'What is it?' Charles Beecher said, 'Why so uptight?'

Washington Smith turned. 'Someone

told Martha.'

'Told Martha what?' There was a hint of accusation in Smith's voice that Beecher didn't like.

Smith walked over to the sideboard and took his time pouring another drink. He turned and stood with his back resting against the sideboard. He sipped the whiskey and stared at Beecher.

'*What?*' Beecher said. The accusation was in Smith's eyes now, as well as his voice. It was the same look he'd had when they'd been discussing killing Jack Anderson. The look of wanting someone dead.

'Evelyn,' Smith said. 'Someone told Martha that Evelyn and I . . . ' Smith shook his head and let the words hang.

'That Evelyn and you are what?' Beecher said.

'Don't pretend you don't know what I'm saying.'

Now Beecher shook his head. It was going bad. Not the business. Far from it, the business was going well. But this — the two of them. They'd always been good together. Their ideas and thought processes aligned. But just recently it felt like the relationship was fractured, like cracks were appearing that if not dealt with might turn into huge fissures.

'It wasn't me,' Beecher said. 'Maybe you want it to be. I don't know. But it wasn't.'

Smith took another sip of whiskey. Then he tilted the glass back and drank all the remainder in one go. He turned to the decanter on the sideboard and refilled the glass to the halfway point.

'It wasn't me,' Beecher said again. 'Makes no difference to me what you get up to. Except maybe your drinking. You're doing way too much of that.'

With his back to Beecher. Smith said, 'Who says I'm getting up to anything?'

'Someone obviously has.'

Smith turned.

'If it wasn't you, who was it?'

'Lord if I know.'

Smith continued to stare at Beecher. Then he sighed, drank another large shot of whiskey and said, 'I'm sorry. I'm on edge. I don't know why. Ever since we killed Anderson.'

'We didn't kill him.'

'We had him killed. I had him killed. I kept on and on and eventually you agreed. And now we've done it and I . . . I don't know, I wake up at night thinking about it.'

'It's done. It's over.'

'Is it?'

'Yes, it is. For good or bad.'

Smith walked back over to the window. It faced out over the yard. He stared aimlessly at the activities below. A locomotive had not long pulled in. The engine still belched steam and smoke. Already his men were swarming over the wagons, un-belting this, looping straps over that, lifting the first of the logs. Elsewhere he could hear the faint screech of wood saws, deadened by the bricks and the thick wooden panelling in the office. The smell of something cooking crept in from somewhere. And over there, high up on the rise north of the site, was a lone rider sitting looking down at him.

'Who's that?' Smith said.

'Where?'

'Come and take a look.'

Beecher joined him at the window.

'It's no one,' Beecher said. 'Just a trail-hand stopping to take a look at the future.'

'He's not moved.'

'Probably smoking a cigarette and resting his horse.'

'I've a spyglass in that drawer over there.'

'Ignore him.'

'Please.' The smell and slur of alcohol came from Smith's mouth. It wasn't the right time to argue.

Beecher opened the drawer that Smith had pointed to. He brought the brass telescope over to Smith. Smith extended the telescope and looked at the distant man.

'Anyone we know?' Beecher said.

'Here take a look.'

Beecher took the telescope and studied the distant rider. It was hard to tell much about him at this distance. A few days of stubble on a weathered and bruised face, a square jaw, eyes shadowed by his hat, and an upright stance on a black horse.

'Means nothing to me,' Beecher said.

'Like I said, I'm just edgy,' Smith said. 'But . . .'

'But what?'

'Last week, for no reason other than we sent Abraham after him, I looked at the photograph of Anderson — Allan — call him what you will. I looked at the rest of them, too.'

'You kept their photographs?'

'I did.'

'There's no way it could be one of them,' Beecher said. 'How would they know?'

'Maybe if they got to Anderson before Abraham? That was the point, wasn't it?'

'You're thinking too hard. We can't even be sure that Anderson knew about us. In fact I doubt he did. You're seeing ghosts where there aren't any.'

'Ghosts I can live with. It's living men

that are bothering me.'

Smith took one last look at the distant rider. He squinted a little as if trying to memorise the man's features, then he turned and walked over to the cabinet from where Beecher had taken the telescope. He opened another drawer and brought out a green leather-covered folder.

Smith said, 'You're probably right. But humour me. Take a look.'

★ ★ ★

The doctor's name was Edward Koch. A short bald man with a great moustache, a beard trimmed to a point, and round wire-framed spectacles. He was dressed well and he laughed loudly. He spoke with a faint European accent and he was clearly fond of Roberta, who had accompanied Rosalie and Leon to Koch's surgery.

'The first thing to do, Mr Winters, is to avoid infecting the rest of us.'

Koch smiled as he spoke, but there

was a seriousness in his eyes. He handed Leon a very soft white folded handkerchief.

'If you get the urge to cough, please cough into that. Outside — you look like an outside man to me — outside, your friends may very well be all right. But in an enclosed space we can't be too careful.'

'Is it catching?' Roberta asked.

'Yes. Yes, it is.'

The girls looked at one another and Leon said, 'Perhaps this isn't a good idea. Perhaps I should go.'

'Nonsense,' Koch said. 'If you want to cough or sneeze just use the handkerchief. Now, you know there's no cure?'

Leon looked at him.

Koch smiled.

'It doesn't mean all is lost, my friend. There are things you can do if you want to live. Now listen closely.'

★　★　★

135

'It could be him,' Beecher said. 'But there again that photograph could be any one of a thousand men in Austin. Especially days when they bring the cattle in.'

The image had been printed on white paper that had become brittle and had cracked in the Texas heat. The cold eyes of a scared young man stared out from the photograph. But, yes, the shape of the jaw and the shoulders, it could have been that rider out there on the ridge.

'I'm being a fool,' Smith said. 'But let's ask the Greek to take a few men and bring him in. Let's see the fellow close up.'

'And if it turns out that it is him?' Beecher asked, tapping the old photograph. He looked again at the picture. 'This Jim Jackson. If it is him. What then?'

Smith thought about this for a moment.

'I'd say we wait and see first. I mean, what are the chances? But we never built all this up by not thinking things through. If it is him. If he's here. Then . . . ' Smith shook his head.

'Abraham?' Beecher said.

'The Greek,' Smith said. 'He'll do it. He's right here. Plus he's a lot cheaper, too.'

★ ★ ★

'Drink milk,' Leon said. 'Eat vegetables.'

'And rest,' Rosalie said.

'One out of three ain't bad,' Leon said.

Roberta looked at him with a quizzical expression.

'I've been living off wild onions this last week,' Leon said and winked.

Roberta smiled. She liked this tall thin man. Partly, she guessed, because he wasn't the one that Rosalie had chased after and had her fingers broken because of. She knew Leon Winters was one of the train robbers that Rosalie had asked her about all those months ago — the only one still alive aside from this Jim Jackson that Rosalie was besotted with. Leon was gracious and chivalrous, almost always smiling — just happy to be alive

137

and free — and it didn't take a detective to figure out that he'd do pretty much anything for Rosalie.

They were walking along Cypress Avenue, slowly wending their way back to Roberta's house. She'd promised them a good meal. They both looked like they needed it.

Rosalie said, 'You need to head west, Leon. The mountains and the dry air. That was the fourth thing.'

'I'm not going anywhere without you.' he said. 'Or Jim.'

'Then we'll come, too.'

Roberta felt a twinge of sadness. Rosalie was always turning up and then leaving. It must be wonderful to have such wanderlust and adventure in one's bones, she thought. Such a carefree and weightless existence. No roots to hold you down. But was it really what Rosalie wanted? Was it really what was best for her? It certainly didn't make life easy for a sister. But, she wondered, was it sadness or jealousy. Rosalie and Leon and Jim, they were all there for each other, and she wasn't really part of it.

Yet as they turned the corner she saw a man standing outside her house and the jealously vanished. She had her own someone, too.

'Andrew's here,' she said to Rosalie. 'I think you'll get on well.' She turned to Leon. 'And he will find you *immensely* interesting, I should think.'

'Why?' Leon asked.

'He's a criminal lawyer. I've told him all about you.'

* * *

It was almost meditative, Jim Jackson decided, although the thought didn't arise until he came out of the dream he had been in. The autumn breeze was warm, but not hot. The sun was hidden behind wispy clouds that took the edge out of the heat. The wild grass smelled fresh and there was birdsong in the air. He could smell coal smoke, too, but it was far enough away for it to feel homely rather than industrial. He was well fed and the ride had been easy, slow and gentle for both him and the horse. There was no rush. He had all day, and although at first he had been worrying about Leon — his health, and the fact that he was venturing into the city — somewhere along the way the worries had vanished and Jim had found himself staring at all the tiny men scurrying about down there in the lumber yard, and his mind had wandered. He thought back to the timber he had set alight as a diversion in order to help Leon escape from the labour camp he was being held in. He thought back to the hundreds of tree-cutting sessions he'd been part of in his own prison. Day after day, month after month. For ten years. Cutting and sawing, dragging and trimming. Hauling heavy timbers along rutted and rocky trails, great ropes around skinny malnourished shoulders. He thought of the times back in Parker's Crossing, New Mexico, where he had run to when first released. He thought of the dark days there when he took refuge in the bottle. And of the men he had killed there. He thought of the friends he still had there. He had saved that town and in the process he had saved himself.

Something brought him out of his reverie and he was disorientated for a moment.

Down below he saw four men riding out of the gate — one of them, a big man on a white and brown pinto — was pointing up at him. As he watched, one of the men cut left, another went right, and the other two — including the big leader — started coming straight towards him.

★ ★ ★

They were in Roberta's small front room — well, it wasn't small, but with Leon and Andrew Beaumont and the two women it felt that way — drinking sweet tea and eating biscuits that Roberta had bought from a baker in town. Leon was still holding the handkerchief that Doctor Koch had given him, but strangely he didn't feel the urge to cough

141

at the moment. It was almost as if just seeing Koch had somehow relieved the symptoms.

'Roberta said she'd told you all about me,' Leon said. He looked briefly across at Roberta, who was sitting on the two-seater alongside Rosalie. 'Should I be worried?'

Beaumont smiled. 'No. You have nothing to worry about.'

'Maybe she hasn't told you everything, then?'

'Maybe I don't know everything,' Roberta said.

'You don't,' Rosalie said. 'Some of it . . . It's too terrible to talk about.'

Roberta looked at her sister. She took one of Rosalie's hands and held it in her lap.

'I'm a lawyer,' Beaumont said. 'Not a marshal or a Texas Ranger, though I know a few of both. But from what Roberta's told me you've served your time.'

'For something I never did,' Leon said. 'Well, I didn't do the worst of what they accused me of.' Leon finally managed a smile. 'I guess everyone says that, though.'

'It's the truth though,' Rosalie said.

'I gather you were in a leasing camp,' Beaumont said.

'Yes.'

'I'm told they are cruel places.'

Leon nodded.

'And I'm not sure they're entirely legal,' Beaumont said. 'At least, in my opinion.'

Leon looked at the lawyer. 'Did you say you knew a Texas Ranger?' he asked.

'Yes, I know several,' Andrew Beaumont said.

★ ★ ★

Jim Jackson jerked the reins hard round to turn the horse. He pressed his spurs into her flanks, and he yelled at her to move. Well rested and full of energy, she leapt forward. Jim hunkered down over her head, out of the wind. He risked a quick look over his shoulder but there was nothing to be seen. The men who had left Beecher and Smith's yard were too far away, down at the bottom of the long slope, or circling far to his left and right.

'*Go! Go!*'

He'd been a fool. Just because Beecher and Smith didn't know him was no reason to think they wouldn't want to investigate someone who was clearly watching their workings. And, of course, they knew of him. That's why they'd had John Allan killed.

'*Faster!*'

His breath came in short bursts as if it was he, rather than the horse, that was doing the hard work. She was already frothing a little at the mouth, but she was strong.

That didn't mean she was stronger than those who were pursuing him.

And they no doubt had geographical knowledge that he lacked. He had ridden slowly, peacefully, towards the general area of Beecher and Smith's, picking up the railroad, and then finding the works. There had been no hurry — Leon and

Rosalie had headed into Austin to see a doctor and probably they would stay overnight. But that meant that if he was caught, maybe dragged back to Beecher and Smith's yard, he'd be on his own.

'Come on!' he urged.

He was riding in a straight line, desperately keeping the sun in the same place over his left shoulder. He figured if he rode straight, then they couldn't outflank him. Not without riding faster than him.

It didn't matter where he went. Just so long as they didn't catch him.

The land was wide open. There was a tree line way over to the west, and rises to the east, somewhere beyond which was Austin. But ahead it was a mile or two of scrubland, where even the grass struggled to grow. Beyond the scrub were the growing shapes of grey hills. If he could get there then he might be able to lose them. He couldn't cut left to the trees — he had to keep racing straight, and he had to keep pushing the horse hard.

Spit was flying back from her mouth now. Her flanks starting to glisten with sweat. Yet already he sensed that her initial sprint was done. She was settling into a fast gallop. Was it enough? He'd never raced her hard and long, wasn't sure of what she was capable.

At one point she stumbled.

If she put a foot in a jackrabbit hole and fell then it was all over.

He noticed that across to his right, and running across his intended path, was a row of fence-posts. He couldn't see if there was any wire strung between the posts, but it was something else to watch out for.

He looked back over his shoulder.

The open grassland was as far behind him now as it was in front. He was in the middle of a lot of nothing, with hardly a tree or a termite mound to hide behind.

The dust from his horse's feet hung in the still air behind him. Then, through the dust, there they were. The two of them who had also ridden straight. Maybe a mile or so back.

Riding fast.

He leaned further over her head. He whispered to her, his words snatched away in the wind that she was creating.

'You can do it,' he said. 'We both can.'

The distant grey hills weren't getting any closer. He thought back to those hills on the ride down earlier. There were thick copses of trees there, a river, rocky outcrops with small gullies and passes. Nothing like the great ranges west of here, but enough to find a hiding place.

If they could get there.

He thought he heard a rifle shot.

It was hard to tell with the wind whistling passed his ears.

If they could get there.

The question was: *what then?* Would simply hiding be enough?

The last time he'd been chased like this, back when he'd broken Leon out of the prison camp, he'd ended up cornering himself in a rocky canyon. He'd come within seconds of being killed that day. He'd planned the ambush reasonably well and would have been fine save for one thing.

He hadn't been able to kill his pursuers in cold blood.

He'd been hidden and he'd had them in his gunsights.

But he'd hesitated, and it was only luck and circumstance that had saved him.

Ahead of him the grey hills finally started to coalesce and thicken. He could see a track leading into them. He started to make out individual trees, the larger rocks. The cover.

'Come on,' he urged. They were going to make it.

But the question remained, as it always did with him: '*What then?*' It had been the same back in Leyton.

He heard a rifle shot again. This time it was unmistakable.

Did it mean they were closer? He risked another look. No, they were still way back out in the middle of the openness. But his horse was slowing, and the wind noise was lessening, and now he could actually see that one of them had a rifle in his hand.

'Keep going!' he pressed his heels harder into her flanks. The froth was flying back from her mouth and neck. She was breathing hard.

The ground began to rise.

What was it Leon had said back in Leyton when they'd had John Allan hooded and tied to a chair?

Give me the word.

Jim hadn't been able to kill John Allan in cold blood, despite all that Allan had put them through. And that reluctance had, just like the events in that canyon by the prison camp, almost led to Jim Jackson's own death.

Leon had been prepared to shoot Allan, but only if Jim had given him the go ahead. And that was akin to pulling the trigger himself. He hadn't even been able to do that.

The upshot was that twice now his failure to be cold-blooded had almost been his downfall.

Yet there had been one time, back in the hide-out after they'd broken Leon out of prison, when he'd had to kill someone in what seemed like, at the time, cold blood. He'd done it, and in the process had saved himself, Leon, and Rosalie.

So he could do it. He told himself that this wasn't Boston. This wasn't the east where a whole set of rules and laws applied. Where good and evil, right and wrong, were set down in law book and statutes and everyone knew where they were.

Sure, Austin was just a few hours ride away, and that place was as civilised as anywhere back east.

But here, out on this range, back in Leyton, in the canyon just south of the prison camp. All of these were wild places. To live and survive here one had to apply a different set of rules. An alternative law-set.

Another bullet whistled by.

He hunkered down as low as he was able.

If they were shooting at him, didn't that give him every right to shoot back?

They were on a rising slope now, almost at the crest. Fifty yards more and they'd be out of sight.

'Just a little further now,' he told her.

Thirty yards.

Twenty.

Another rifle shot and this time the horse stumbled.

For a moment Jim thought it was the loose scree beneath her feet. She appeared to find balance and momentum again, but then he saw blood in the air, spraying back from somewhere. Her legs buckled and it was only reflexes that kept him from being trapped beneath her as she fell.

He landed hard on the ground.

The horse was looking at him. There was a plea for assistance in her wide scared eyes.

'I'm sorry,' he said.

He grabbed a water skin from the back of the saddle and sprinted to the shelter of the nearest rise.

* * *

'Can I read it?' Andrew Beaumont said.

151

Leon shrugged. 'Why not? You can tell me what you think.'

Beaumont unfolded the piece of paper that Leon had been writing on. He read the words and was quiet for a few moments.

He looked at Leon.

'Are you sure you want to do this?'

'I can't think of any other way.'

'They could simply arrest you.'

'For what? I did my time. Jim did his.'

'Except you didn't, did you? Jim broke you out of prison. They'd be well within their rights to arrest you both. They love Texas more than anything. You know that?'

'Do they believe in the truth?'

Andrew Beaumont smiled. 'Like I said, they love Texas more than anything.'

'Jim foiled a train robbery,' Rosalie said. 'I was there.'

'I know. Roberta told me.'

'He's on the side of . . . good,' Rosalie said.

'Well. I'll pass it on. How will I get word back to you?'

'I've promised to stay,' Rosalie said. 'For a day or two. I'll take the reply back to the boys.'

Andrew Beaumont looked at Leon again.

'Sure?'

Leon felt that tickle in his throat again. It seemed like the respite from simply seeing Doctor Koch was over. He raised the handkerchief to his mouth and coughed, feeling and tasting the blood in his throat.

'I'm sure,' he said.

★ ★ ★

It was time to learn the lesson. Not third time lucky, but third time *unlucky*. For someone.

That occasion in the canyon south of the prison camp was number one. The situation with John Allan in Leyton, number two. This wasn't Sunday school. If you kept avoiding the hard truth out here you would die. It was that simple.

They'd shot his horse and they were,

presumably, happy to shoot him, too.

So lesson learned.

This time he would come out shooting.

9

Jim Jackson had the sun behind him. It had been accidental, rather than planned. But it worked well and he would remember it in future.

He lay just below the top of the rise, his head behind a rock, and he peered through the long grass at the two horsemen.

Jim figured the one in the lead was the fellow in charge. He couldn't be sure, but he thought it was that one who had been giving out the orders when the four riders had first left the yard gates.

The man was big, with wide shoulders and a great belly — maybe that was what had saved Jim from being caught back there in the open. The man's horse looked exhausted. Behind him rode a smaller, leaner man. This one with the rifle in his hand. He was scanning the area, and he looked tense and ready to drop the reins from his left hand, steady the rifle, and shoot down Jim the moment he saw movement.

Back before any of this had started, before Jim had even suspected there was anything other than bad luck that had got him incarcerated for ten years, the Texas Ranger Sam McRae, had said to some folks in Parker's Crossing, New Mexico, that there was no doubting Jim Jackson was the quickest gunman that McRae had ever seen in Texas. McRae had said this in the moments before Jim Jackson had a gunfight. Jim had never figured out how Sam McRae had known how fast he was. And, on reflection, he wondered if McRae had said it just to give Jim a little more confidence in those stomach-churning moments before the shoot-out. However, there was no denying that he was fast. He knew that. He'd never really worked at it. It just came naturally.

The thing was that right now it didn't matter. Indeed in most cases it never mattered. It was rarely about speed.

It was always about the willingness to

kill.

And that had been Jim Jackson's weakness.

Had been, he said aloud.

The two riders were barely twenty yards away.

Jim stood up, gun already drawn.

His first bullet took the thin man in the chest, lifted him off his saddle and out of his stirrups. Even before the man had hit the ground Jim adjusted his aim and shot the big man twice. The man was still turning, still trying to focus on Jim Jackson, his mouth opening to say something when the bullets ploughed into him, almost as one. There was an explosion of red mist as the bullets exited the man's back. But he was too big to be blown off the horse. His eyes widened, his mouth, too. A bubble of blood rose and burst from his lips, and he slid off the horse, slowly, like a huge bag of feed that hadn't been tied on tight. The horse accelerated in fear and dragged the big man several yards before the man's right foot broke loose from the stirrup and he lay motionless on the ground, dust rising up around him.

Jim Jackson's breath came in rapid bursts, almost as quick as his shooting had been. First he breathed through his mouth. Then the breathing became sniffle and sobs and he breathed through his nose. Then he took deep breaths and blew the air out of his mouth, trying to calm himself, slow his racing heart, and control the rising sickness in his belly.

'You shouldn't have been shooting at me,' he said. As if speaking it aloud might make everything all right. 'You shouldn't have been shooting at me.'

But the words didn't make it all right.

Whichever way he looked at it, he was now a killer. A stone killer. Not a killer in self-defence, not a killer protecting someone else, just a killer.

He dropped his gun and he fell to his knees. He bowed his head and then a moment later he looked Heavenwards.

'What have I become?'

But there was no answer.

158

* * *

Ike Landreth heard the gunshots. Initially they were intermittent. Maybe a minute or two apart. Then there was nothing. He wondered if maybe Billy or the Greek had shot the fellow they said was spying on the yard. But then came three more shots. Three in such quick succession that there may actually have only been two.

Shots so rapid they must have come from a revolver.

Landreth felt a cold hand wrap itself around his spine and start to squeeze.

Earlier, the Greek had told him to get his horse saddled up and to be over at the gate as quickly as he could. 'We've got a fellow to bring in. Mr Smith wants to talk to him.'

'What's he done?'

'Spying.'

Then the Greek had added, 'Bring your rifle.'

Landreth had been working at Beecher and Smith's for a few months now. It was easy work. He was just a deputy to the Greek's sheriff. They weren't really deputy and sheriff. They had no authority, of course. Not outside the yard. But within it, well that was a different matter. There were so many people there now, working, living, playing. Women, too. They had a saloon and there was rotgut whiskey brewed on site. Gambling and a little whoring went on. And most nights there were fights, mostly fistfights, but sometime with knives, and just occasionally someone would draw a gun. A lot of money came in, too. Wages for all of those workers. So there was always lots to do, keeping everyone safe and calm, and maybe knocking down a few men if they got too rowdy, and even locking them up in the makeshift jail. It would have been a hell of a job for one man. One man, whoever he was, probably wouldn't have lasted a week, but for four of them, especially with the Greek in charge, it was pretty easy. They'd had to set a few examples earlier on, but now that folks knew where they stood, and what they could get away with it, it was easy work.

Easy enough that this, chasing down someone from outside the yard, was an exciting break from the norm.

The Greek had sent him left, saying that he was to ride as hard as he could and ride along the tree line where they'd killed those coyotes a month before. 'You'll see us trailing him,' the Greek had said. 'If he cuts towards you, don't be afraid to shoot him. Maybe his horse. Whichever. The fellow's up there spying. There's no good reason for that.'

That was the thing about the Greek. He took no messing. Hell, he was as vicious as the worst of them. Landreth had seen him break a man's arm, and he'd heard stories that the Greek had killed men, too. That's why the job was so easy in the yard, even on the wildest of Saturday nights. Landreth had rarely had to do anything other than be there and be ready to back up the Greek.

The Greek had sent young Kansas Joe to ride the fence line on the right-hand edge of the plain. Whichever way the spy rode, they'd get him sooner or later.

But those three shots.

They sounded awfully quick.

★ ★ ★

Jim Jackson was tying his own bag to the back of the horse on which the thin guy had been riding when he saw the man bearing down on him from the east. The man, on horseback, was holding a revolver, and his face was pulled into an anguished grimace. He was no more than fifty yards away and even as Jim noticed him the man started to blaze away with his gun. Once, twice. Three times. The horse was at full gallop and Jim had no idea where the man's bullets went. He dived onto the floor, and then scrambled to the other side of the horse, putting all that heavy horseflesh between himself and the rider.

The man was screaming now.

Jim risked a look around the back of the horse's rump. He held onto the stirrup

162

on his side of the horse with his left hand and said, 'Easy boy.' The horse was obviously used to gun fire, but he didn't want it suddenly panicking, bolting off, and leaving him in plain sight.

'Easy.'

The man was thirty yards away.

Now twenty.

The man fired twice more, and this time Jim heard the whistle of a bullet in the air.

Now the man was upon him, his horse bursting past the one that Jim hid behind. The rider heaving on the reins, the horse skidding, going down on his knees, finding its feet again in a cloud of dust, rising, turning, shrieking, and the rider twisting towards Jim, a young face full of wild anger, cursing Jim, his gun steadier now, and Jim standing with one hand holding his horse's stirrup and the other resting on its flank, his own gun, picked up earlier from where he'd dropped it, back in its holster, where Jim had just moments before sworn never to use it again.

The boy, for he looked no older than seventeen or eighteen, looked at Jim, called him a word that Jim wouldn't even use himself, and pulled the trigger.

Jim saw the flames and smoke explode from the gun.

He felt the bullet punch him in the left-hand shoulder, spinning him back against the horse, and in the process freeing his right hand and his gun, which had both been pressed up against the horse.

The boy squeezed the trigger again. This time there was nothing but a dry click.

A look of panic flashed across the boy's eyes. But then he blinked, dropped the handgun, and was already heaving a rifle from a saddle scabbard.

Jim drew his revolver.

He shot the boy in the chest.

There was a look of surprise and disbelief on the boy's face and then he fell backwards off the horse and was still.

★　★　★

Ike heard more shooting. Lots of shooting. One, two, three. Four, Five. A pause, then six.

And seven.

He'd lost sight of the men on the plain earlier, but that was OK as he knew where he was headed. Now he paused on the edge of the tree line looking out over the grasslands, his stomach churning.

There was nothing to see. Not from here.

He was going to have to ride into the open.

* * *

Jim Jackson wept silently and without realising it, as he finished tying his belongings to the thin man's saddle. He wept as he reloaded his gun. He was still weeping as he mounted the horse and called for her to run.

He was aware that there was a fourth man out there, just as he'd been aware that there had been a third man. But the way he was feeling he might just let the man shoot him and have done with it all, the agony, the guilt, everything.

Killing the first two had left him numb and unable to think.

Killing the third had filled that emptiness inside him with a terrible searing guilt.

His shoulder burned and pain radiated out like flames from a fire. It was good pain. It was pain he deserved. He could feel the blood soaking his shirt. Let me bleed, he thought. Maybe he even said it aloud. He wasn't sure.

Then he told himself that it was them — *they* had been shooting at him. They had shot his horse. And in this new world that he found himself, had he not done what he did, then it would have been third time unlucky. He'd be dead.

Yet the argument, and the resolutions he'd made about third time *unlucky* before the killings, didn't stop the anguish in his heart or the churning in his belly. If one could drown in guilt, he thought, then I'd be at the bottom of the

Missouri, and then some.

The internal argument raged as he rode north, bleeding and crying, weakening from blood loss and not caring about a fourth man — if that man appeared then so be it. And he watched himself from afar, as if somehow his soul had become separated from his body.

Maybe it has, he told himself.

Maybe it has.

* * *

Ike Landreth found the Greek's body, and not far away was Kansas Joe lying with his eyes open, a look of surprise on his young face as if he couldn't believe that the world didn't do just as he asked, which was the way back in the yard because everyone knew the Greek had Joe's back. But out here nobody had told that to the rest of the world.

There was a dead horse, too. Not a horse that Landreth recognized.

And over there, was Slim.

Slim's horse was gone, the other two

horses were standing a few yards away, not grazing, just standing there looking as if they couldn't believe it either.

Landreth realised there were tears on his cheek.

'Son of a bitch,' he said.

He looked to the north. There was still dust in the air. The day had become still. Still enough that a man could follow that dust trail if he was quick. And if he cared to.

But he looked back at the bodies of his friends and he knew that he didn't care to track the man that had done it.

He would tie the bodies to the horses and he would take them back to the yard.

And after that, who knew?

10

'My God,' Leon said.

He was back in their camp, hidden in the woods, up against the protection of the rock face. There was a fire burning, with a pot of coffee standing on the flat rock overhanging the flames, and a rabbit carcass skewered on a stick roasting above the flames. Leon's bedroll was unrolled, ready for the coming darkness.

Jim Jackson eased his horse — a different horse, Leon noticed — to the edge of the camp where Leon's horse was eating grass.

Leon leapt to his feet and just made it across to Jim before the latter slid sideways off his saddle. Leon caught Jim and lowered him to the ground.

Jim grunted in pain, looked up at Leon, and smiled.

'How's the cough, partner? You cured?'

'Seems to me you're the one needs the doctor. My God, what happened?'

Leon helped Jim to his feet and then supported him across to the fire.

'You've been shot.'

'Bullet went straight through,' Jim said. 'I was lucky. Not what I deserved.'

'Let me look.'

Leon undid Jim's jacket and shirt. Jim shivered in the cooling shaded air. Leon washed the wound. It was still seeping a little blood, but already the worst of the wound, both front and back was congealing. If Jim could lie still for long enough he might be OK. With nothing to clean or bandage the wound with, all Leon could do was redress Jim and have him lie down as close to the fire as he could. He gave Jim coffee and rabbit meat.

'I didn't catch it. I bought it from a feller on the way out of Austin.'

'You didn't get recognized then.'

'We need to take you there.'

'No. I'll be fine.'

'What happened, Jim?'

'Where's Rosalie?'

'Rosalie will be here tomorrow. Maybe the day after. She's spending the time with her sister.'

Jim looked up at Leon with questions in his eyes.

'She's fine. I'm fine.' Although even as he spoke Leon was trying desperately not to cough. The way the consumption was now, once he started he was finding it harder to stop. Vegetables and milk, warm dry weather, and rest. So much for any of that.

Jim's eyes closed.

'I shot them,' Jim said. 'Three of them.'

Leon covered him with a blanket.

'Who.'

'Don't know. They were shooting at me first.'

'Then it's nothing to feel guilty about.'

'You weren't there.'

'I know you, Jim.'

Jim's eyes flickered open. 'I'm not sure I know myself anymore.'

★ ★ ★

That night Jim flickered in and out of consciousness. Leon sat awake feeding

171

the fire and, during his partner's lucid moments, feeding Jim warm roasted rabbit and hot water, coffee and biscuits. In the morning he checked the bullet wound in Jim's shoulder. A night of lying reasonably still meant the bleeding had stopped. But there was no doubting Jim had lost a lot of blood. His shirt was as hard as leather where the blood had soaked in and dried.

'You want to talk about it?' Leon asked at one point.

'No,' Jim said, but half an hour later, his eyes closed, he started mumbling about how they shouldn't have shot his horse. They shouldn't have been shooting at him. What was a man to do? Sooner or later a man's luck would run out, Jim said, and so that man had to come out shooting.

Leon knew that Jim had lost a horse before, one of which he had been extremely fond. The horse that had carried Jim in endless scouting missions as he had tried to figure out a way of getting Leon out of prison. Maybe that had been the trigger. Hell, most men would come out shooting if you killed their horse.

And if the guys were shooting at Jim himself, what did they expect? Leon recalled their days more than ten years before when they had brought trains to a halt by putting great logs or rocks on the tracks and how Jim had walked through the carriages, never ever needing to use his gun in anger, but once or twice drawing and firing at lightning speed, maybe shooting a hole in the centre of a clock or a face on a poster. Just enough to make everyone aware of how good he was. Then they'd collect their hard-earned stealings.

Those horsemen, whoever they had been, would have had no idea of who they were dealing with.

Leon stood up to get another log from the pile he had built up. He coughed into his hand, then he spat blood out into the undergrowth. The pain in his chest was worsening. When he coughed now it felt like there was a rusty blade in his throat. It was one thing the doc telling him to eat well, rest, and find a warm dry climate. It was another thing to actually be in a position to do those things.

'Maybe they only wanted to talk,' Jim said.

Leon turned. The low flames gave the stones around the fire an orange sheen, but by the time the light got to Jim it had turned grey.

'They don't shoot your horse if they just want to talk.'

But Jim's eyes were closed. He was dreaming or hallucinating.

'Same as the boy in the woods,' Jim said, and his face contorted, not in pain, but with a bad memory.

'You had no choice,' Leon said. But wasn't he just like that doctor? Giving advice that the recipient was in no position to take?

He put a log on the fire and pulled the blanket tight around his own throat. The morning felt damp and even breathing was starting to hurt now.

* * *

'Someone's approaching,' Jim said.

Leon took up station behind some trees on the far side of the camp, and Jim, sitting up now, had his Colt already drawn beneath the blanket that was wrapped around him.

Then they heard Rosalie singing quietly, her voice sweet and tuneful.

'It's me,' she said, stopping her horse where the other horses were tethered and grazing, letting them nuzzle each other in greetings.

Jim heard her say to one of the horses. 'You're new. Where did you come from?'

She stepped into the camp.

'What on earth . . .'

She ran to Jim and went to hug him, but his expression stopped her. She pulled back the blanket and saw the blood, the gun. She looked at his face and saw the pain and the paleness beneath his beard, and the blue and purple bruises that John Allan had given him.

She looked across at Leon.

He looked equally as tired as Jim. There was blood on his chin of which he was unaware.

'I . . . I . . . ' She fumbled for words.

'Morning,' Jim said, and smiled.

'I leave you boys for two days,' she said. 'And look what happens.'

★ ★ ★

Rosalie had bought two new shirts in Austin, a pair of new pants, too. She told the men how Roberta has wanted her to buy blouses and skirts, fancy shoes.

'She was horrified when all I bought — well, she bought them as a present — were trousers that, in her words, a man would wear. And the shirts are actually men's shirts. I think she was trying to seduce me into staying in the city.'

Rosalie tore her old shirt into several strips. She soaked one torn sleeve in warm water and washed Jim's wound best she could, then she made two compresses out of the rear of the torn shirt and bound these in place. One of her new shirts fitted Jim, so they threw his blood-soaked shirt on the fire, where it flared and smoked and smelled like something evil had inhabited it.

She'd brought food again, including meat, vegetables and a bottle of milk ('for Leon'), and she rustled up a dinner that Jim said wouldn't have been amiss in a restaurant.

'When did you last go to a restaurant?' Rosalie asked.

'The day after I met you,' he said, smiling.

Jim told them what had happened, unaware that he'd already told Leon much of it, of how he'd been sitting staring at Beecher and Smith's operation, simply letting his mind wander, when the men had come after him.

'Who are they?' Leon said. 'I mean, Beecher and Smith? I know *who* they are. But . . . you know, who are they?'

'I don't know. But it's all connected.'

'Could they have recognized you?'

'I don't see how. I was a long way away. And as far as I know I've never met them in my life.'

'I've got some news,' Rosalie said. 'From Andrew.'

'Who's Andrew?' Jim asked.

'Andrew,' Leon said, 'is Rosalie's sister's boyfriend. He knows some Texas Rangers.'

Jim thought back to a conversation that Leon and he had had a few days previously. He looked at Leon and then back at Rosalie.

'Go on.'

'They want to meet you,' Rosalie said. 'The Texas Rangers. One of them, anyway.'

'That's crazy,' Jim said. 'I'm a wanted man. We're all wanted.'

'Hear me out.'

'OK. I'm listening.'

'Andrew — Roberta's boyfriend — said that the Texas Ranger concerned is a man by the name of Will Baker.'

'So?'

'Andrew said he would vouch for Baker's honesty and integrity. He assured me that if Baker made a promise to meet you under a flag of truce, as it were, then he would honour that.'

A pulse of pain came from Jim's shoulder. He grimaced.

'I'm to trust a lawman because a fellow I've never met, and am unlikely ever to meet, says the lawman is trustworthy. Hell, he doesn't even know anything about me. About us.'

'Yes he does,' Leon said.

'What have you two been plotting?' Jim said. He shook his head, closed his eyes, and laughed thinly. 'I'm sorry. My shoulder hurts. I feel like hell. Go on. I shall listen with open ears and an open mind.'

Leon said, 'I told him that Sam McRae knew something. And I told him that the Ranger that was killed on that train ten years ago —'

'More.'

'Well, I told him ten years.'

'You've met him, this Texas Ranger?'

'I wrote a letter.'

'How did I miss all this?'

'You were out getting shot,' Rosalie said.

179

'And shooting,' Jim said. He pursed his lips as if the thought needed further consideration.

'I told him there was something about that Ranger on the train. That it wasn't random.'

'And he wants to meet you,' Rosalie said.

'Just me?'

'He said, one to one would probably seem fairest to you.'

'Where and when is this meeting?'

'Tomorrow at noon. There's a flatland not far from here — it's coincidence, he doesn't know where we're camped. Are you going to be strong enough?'

Jim closed his eyes. He nodded to himself. They were good people, Leon and Rosalie. He'd gone riding down there, looking at Beecher and Smith directly and had ended up close to being killed and having to kill men just to escape. And they, his friends, carefully and subtly came at it from a different and far better direction.

'I've never felt better,' Jim said.

11

Washington Smith said, 'Wire Abraham. Tell him to come.'

Charles Beecher looked at Evelyn and nodded. She wasn't waiting for any go ahead from Beecher — she was Smith's secretary and would do what she was told — but Beecher could see hesitancy in her eyes. Neither of them had ever seen Smith so mad, so incensed.

Evelyn went out and closed the door.

Smith turned to Beecher.

'What's going on? What the hell is going on?'

'Maybe nothing,' Beecher said. 'Landreth reckoned the Greek was shooting at that fellow first, whoever he was. Hell, Washington. There's probably not a man working for us who wouldn't shoot to kill you if you were shooting at him first. Doesn't mean anything's going on.'

'That Greek. Headfirst, always. I told him to bring the man in. Not kill him.'

'Landreth seemed to think the Greek may have been shooting at the fellow's horse. But for most men that's the same as being shot at.'

Smith looked at Beecher. Then he turned and walked over to the sideboard where the whiskey decanter stood, almost empty, almost time for it to be refilled. Again. There was broken glass on the floor where Smith had hurled a whiskey glass earlier. Evelyn had swept up as much glass as she could see, but Smith had been mad and it hadn't been the time for fastidious cleaning.

'No,' Smith said, pouring all the remaining whiskey into a glass. 'Something is going on. I feel it in my bones.'

'Who are we going to set Abraham on this time?'

'Anyone who comes.'

★　★　★

The morning was cool, a definite sense of fall in the air. Away from the tree line a low ground mist covered the grass, making the trail hard to see. The shadows created by the rising sun were very long and the sky was awash with gorgeous reds and oranges.

'We'll ride with you to the edge of the flatland,' Leon said.

'Sure.' Jim smiled reassuringly.

Rosalie had cleaned and bandaged the bullet wound again that morning. It hurt. Every time he breathed it hurt. Every step the horse took it hurt. But he figured the smile hid that hurt well.

'Are you sure you want to do this?' Rosalie asked.

'When I tried the alternative I ended up with a bullet in my shoulder.'

'I can go instead,' Leon said. 'I was there on the train. I heard what Allan had to say. I know the story.'

'No. It's my place to do this. I was with Sam McRae. If we want to know the truth about what's really going on we have to trust someone. Baker sounds as good as anyone. Come on. Let's go.'

★ ★ ★

Where the trees ended, where the land opened up into a great rolling plain and where the light wind rippled the low grass like waves on a lake, they paused again. There were cattle grazing out there on the flats, and a buzzard circled lazily above them. The air smelled clean and the breeze felt good on their faces.

'You've better eyesight than me,' Leon said. 'Do you see him?'

'Not yet.'

'We'll be right here.'

'I'll be right there,' Jim said, nodding to the flatland where there was nowhere to hide, no place to run.

Jim looked back at Rosalie. 'I won't be long.' Then he heeled his horse and walked her forward into the open, to meet a Texas lawman.

* * *

'You're taking a risk,' Will Baker said. 'You're a wanted man. I mean, you're one of *the* wanted men. There's more than a little money on your head.'

184

Jim Jackson looked across at the Texas Ranger. Baker was sitting aside a fine grey. He had a rifle in a saddle scabbard, and he was wearing a six-gun.

'How much?' Jim asked.

'Five hundred dollars.'

Jim whistled. 'Are you tempted?'

'If *I* bring you in I don't get a penny.'

'Just glory,' Jim said.

'Uh-huh. Just glory.'

Baker smiled. He looked to be in his forties, clean shaven with a tanned and wind-weathered face. The brim of his hat cast a half-shadow over his eyes, but what Jim could see of those eyes they were clear and bright.

Jim looked across the clearing. There was no one else to be seen. No Rosalie, no Leon, and no other Rangers. His heart was pounding. In many ways this was scarier than standing up in a gunfight. At least Jim knew he could hold his own in such a thing. Here it was all about words, all about trying to make someone understand what had happened and why. It was about discovery,

185

too. And maybe that was the scariest thing. What if he'd laid himself on the line this way and there was nothing to be learned. Who was to say Baker, this man that Roberta's boyfriend vouched for, actually knew anything?

Baker said, 'But then I've brought in more than my fair share of train robbers and murderers already. I don't need any more glory.'

'That's a relief.'

'It doesn't mean I won't take you in.'

Jim wanted to say that Baker could try, that it was by no means a foregone conclusion. But he resisted. Will Baker held all the aces. Hell, he had all the cards. It was not a moment for being antagonistic.

'I thought we were here under an agreement of truce?'

'We are. But there's always tomorrow.'

Jim smiled. 'I don't deny I'm a train robber. But I did my time. And then some. Murderer? All I ask is that you listen to what I have to say before making your mind up on that one.'

'According to the record pinned up at the depot you killed four men in a gulley just south of the prison camp from where you broke out a serving prisoner. A prison guard and a railroad guard are both missing — most everyone assumes you killed them both and buried the bodies. More recently we hear that a sheriff and three deputies were shot dead up in Leyton. That's . . . I don't know. I've already lost count. And that's not including two train robbers you shot dead right here in Austin. It seems to me that you're a one-man killing spree. But go on, I'm listening.'

The sun felt hot on Jim's neck. His throat was dry and dusty. Will Baker was wrong. Jim hadn't killed all those men he had listed — but he'd killed enough of them, and now he found himself breathing heavily through his open mouth, and wondering if actually he was a cold-blooded killer. There had been others, too. Back in New Mexico. Surely a man wouldn't leave so many people dead if he was a good man?

'There's talk of something else, too,' Baker said. 'Washington Smith, from . . . ' He waved his hand in the general direction of the distant trees to his right. 'From the lumber yard. Talk is he lost three men, two days ago. Shot dead.'

Jim Jackson said nothing, but he held Baker's stare.

'You see,' Baker said. 'The way I'm thinking is that this has something to do with Washington Smith and that means those three men are most likely not a coincidence. And that in turns mean you may have killed more men than just about anyone I've ever come across.'

There it was again. Baker wasn't totally wrong. The numbers couldn't lie. Surely a good person wouldn't have needed to kill so many men.

'I never killed anyone who wasn't trying to kill me first,' Jim said. 'On that I swear.'

'You must have a lot of enemies.'

'That's what I'm trying to find out.'

Baker nodded, as if the statement dovetailed into something he already knew.

'They told me you knew Sam McRae,' Jim said.

'Uh-huh.'

'This gun . . . ' Jim held his hand out down by his side, careful to keep his hand well clear from the holster. 'This was McCrae's gun. The men that killed him. I avenged his death.'

'Parker's Crossing, New Mexico,' Will Baker said. 'Sam was doing a little bounty hunting. I know what happened. More killings . . . But they speak highly of you there.'

'You've been there?'

'Not personally.'

'He was hunting some bad men. But that wasn't the only reason he was there. He came to find me. To apologise to me.'

'I know.'

'You know?'

'Sam wrote it all down. We all write down what we're doing. Sam kept that habit even after he'd left the Rangers. We're trained to record things. Well, most things anyway. Right now, this meeting isn't written down anywhere.'

Jim Jackson paused for a moment, trying to figure if that was a good thing or not.

'He was the one that arrested me.'

'I was there.'

'You were there? I don't — '

'I was young. I was like . . . You know, a young boy just setting out on his first cattle drive. Come back in ten or twelve years' time and you won't recognize him.'

'So you know *why* Sam came to apologise.'

'I do now. It's the only reason I'm here. The only reason I'm sitting and listening.'

'We were set up,' Jim said. 'All of us.'

'By a fellow called Jack Anderson in Leyton. The man you killed just over a week ago.'

'You knew about him?'

'I didn't know the connection until yesterday when Andrew Beaumont came to see me. I hadn't looked up Sam's notes before. No one had. They were covered in dust and the ink was fading, but they were readable.'

'What did they say?'

'Nothing you don't already know. You were arrested for train robbery and murder. It was a straightforward arrest. Later on he added a note that you were found guilty and that you'd been sent to Huntsville. You were lucky not to hang. I think maybe the judge knew it was all wrong.'

Baker twisted in his saddle and lifted his water skin. He drank thirstily. Jim Jackson took the opportunity to take some of his own water. It felt cool and clean. His shoulder was throbbing and he could feel sweat running down his back and sides.

'But you know more than that,' Jim said. 'Now.'

'Sam wrote that he was convinced you were innocent. That witnesses were adamant. But the jury found you guilty and there was nothing more —'

'Someone should talk to those jurors. It never added up.'

'Sam tended to agree. But it wasn't

his place. It never got done.'

Baker had kept hold of his water skin. He took another drink.

'Anyway, just before he left us, he added another note. The one about Jack Anderson. I don't know how Sam found out about Anderson, but there it was. Sam had written, *I think this is the man we should be looking at.* I even wonder if that's why he went solo — so he could go and make those investigations himself.'

'John Allan — sorry, Jack Anderson. They're one and the same. He admitted to me that he had killed the Texas Ranger on that train all those years ago.'

'Just before you killed him?'

'I was tied up. He was going to hang me in the morning. He was gloating.'

'I know.'

'You know?'

'The letter Andrew Beaumont gave me. The one your friend Leon wrote.'

'Then you know he did it for a reason. I mean, John Allan. You know John Allan killed that Texas Ranger for a reason.'

'The Texas Ranger was named Riley

King. Folks knew him as So-So King. They said he put the nickname out there himself. He let it be known that he was only so-so with a gun. Actually, they say, he was the best. And all those people who went up against him thinking that he was just so-so. Well they lived to regret it. But generally not for very long.'

'Riley King,' Jim said, picturing the man rising up in that carriage all those years ago, turning smiling, full of confidence that he could take on this entire band of train robbers singlehandedly. The moment that started everything.

'Leon's letter said that you and he figured Riley wasn't shot at random and that we should be looking at Beecher and Smith for a reason.'

'Did you look?'

'Oh yes.'

'And did you find anything?' Jim asked.

* * *

193

Jim said to Leon and Rosalie, 'Riley's papers were even more dusty and faded than McRae's had been. No one had really looked at them on account of his killing had seemed so random. Oh they'd checked, just in case there was a connection, but Riley wasn't a writer, wasn't fastidious, and most of the good stuff had been on scraps of paper that had just been put in a box.'

'And?' Rosalie said.

'It turns out that Riley King was suspicious that something was going on with the leasing system.'

'The prisoner leasing system? Where you both ended up?' Rosalie said.

They were riding slowly back through the woods, towards their camp.

'Yes. But this was before we'd even been arrested. I don't know what had triggered Riley King's interest but he'd noticed that an awful lot of the men that were being sent to leasing camps were being sent to camps run by — or rather owned by — or supplying lumber to Beecher and Smith.'

'*Cheap* lumber,' Leon said.

'So he started digging,' Jim said. 'He talked to Beecher and Smith. He talked to three commissioners who sat on the prison board — essentially the ones that made the decision as to who went where. They all denied it. But there was something there. That's what he wrote: *There's something here that smells.*'

Leon shook his head in wonderment.

'So they had John Allan kill him.'

'Yep, looks that way. Maybe the commissioners pressurised Beecher and Smith, or maybe they did it off their own accord. Maybe all three commissioners were in on it, or maybe only two. Baker said he had no idea how Beecher and Smith knew that Riley King would be on that train. The other thing was that someone knew all about our gang and yet we hadn't been arrested. It was like that somebody had figured we might be worth keeping out there. And sure enough it turned out we were. Baker says he'll figure all this out eventually.'

Leon said, 'So John Allan killed King,

we were arrested, and King's investigation came to a grinding halt.'

'Yep.'

'And all was fine until you were released, and you broke me free,' Leon said.

'Yep.'

'And suddenly Beecher and Smith started to get nervous.'

'I think we were meant to die in the system,' Jim said.

'Everyone else did. I think — I don't know — but I think that's why we were treated the way we were. They were trying to kill us without it looking like murder.'

'My God,' Rosalie said.

'Indeed. Money talks . . . Maybe they paid the jurors? If they could do that, then it's only a small step to paying a couple of leasing camp guards to slowly kill us.'

'But we lived,' Leon said.

'And the only other person who knew the story, or at least part of it, was Allan. And suddenly they were worried that we might track him down — '

'Which we did.'

'And he might tell us what really happened.'

'Which he did.'

'Why didn't they kill John Allan before?' Rosalie said.

'I don't know. Baker doesn't know. Maybe they figured that if Allan died suddenly it would look too suspicious.'

Leon said, 'That's why they sent out men to kill you. They recognized you and — '

'I don't think so,' Jim said. 'I doubt they would have recognized me at that distance. That's even assuming they know me. I think they are just very scared all of a sudden.'

'So,' Rosalie said. 'What happens now?'

'It's about to get very interesting indeed,' Jim said.

12

There were four Texas Rangers, including Will Baker. There was Jim Jackson, and Leon Winters. And there was Rosalie Robertson. Baker wasn't happy about Jim, Leon, and Rosalie being in attendance, but after some debate he had acquiesced. Beecher and Smith were just business men, he said. He didn't anticipate any trouble, and just maybe the fact that Jim and Leon were there might help. 'Maybe it'll put them off-balance. Maybe they'll say something in haste that they'll live to regret in leisure,' he'd said.

They rode slowly along the trail towards the lumber yard, riding alongside the railroad spur, and then cutting onto the hard-packed road.

It was morning, not too hot even though it was a very still day.

Jim looked across at Leon.

'It's hard to believe it all comes to this — this yard, these two people.'

'And a couple or three politicians,' Leon said.

The gates of the lumber yard became visible in the distance.

'These two will sing like birds,' Jim said. He nodded at the back of Will Baker who was riding about twenty yards ahead of them. 'According to Will, anyway. They'll give the commissioners up.'

'Just so long as they don't escape justice themselves,' Rosalie said.

'Won't happen,' Jim said. 'No one likes thieves and liars. But men in power who use that power in evil ways . . . They're the worst. That's Will speaking, by the way. But I agree with him.'

'Everything that happened,' Leon said, looking at the distant lumber yard. 'It could all have been avoided.'

'We weren't innocent,' Jim said. 'And anyway . . . ' He smiled at Rosalie. 'I probably wouldn't change a thing.'

Ahead of them Will raised a hand and everyone stopped.

The Ranger turned.

'OK, this is what we're going to do.'

Smith was drinking when Beecher came into the office. The tall bearded gunslinger, Abraham, was sitting at Smith's table.

'They're here,' Beecher said.

Smith turned.

'Who?'

'Seven of them. You can see them at the gate from the window in my office.'

'Seven?'

'Yep.'

'Armed?' Smith said.

Abraham looked over. 'Of course they'll be armed.' One of his own guns was on the table in front of him. He picked it up and spun the cylinder. He smiled at Beecher.

'Maybe we should talk to them first,' Beecher said. 'We don't know what they want.'

'Abraham here was just telling me that back up in Leyton our friend Jack Anderson had plenty of time to talk to Jim Jackson and Leon Winters.' Smith held up the faded photos of the two train robbers. 'And he's confirmed it was Jackson and Winters who were up there. I'm betting Anderson did some digging of his own over the years. Found out who we were.'

'Why would Anderson have told them anything?' Beecher asked.

'Men like to boast,' Abraham said. 'He had those fellows caged. Was going to hang them. I guess he might have wanted to let them know just how clever he was.'

'And they escaped.'

'I shot Anderson. Just like you two paid me to. If you'd have told me the full story I could have shot those other fellows, too. Then you wouldn't be in this mess.'

'So they know everything?'

'We don't know,' Smith said. 'But I guess we'll find out when we talk to them.'

'And if they do know everything?'

Abraham spun the cylinder on his Colt again. And smiled.

* ★ ★

The man at the gate was a short fellow with a wide-brimmed hat, a black vest over a white shirt, and a rifle in his hand.

'Hold on,' he said, when he saw the riders approaching.

'Just hold on there.'

Will Baker raised a hand, the reins resting lightly between his thumb and fingers.

'Don't recognize you,' the gateman said. 'And you don't look like no lumber dealers.'

'What does a lumber dealer look like?' Will asked.

'Normally the fellow wears a suit. Makes him look important, like.'

Will nodded.

'We're important. We've come to see Mr Beecher and Mr Smith.'

'Important, huh? Who are you?'

'Tell him the Texas Rangers are here.'

★ ★ ★

The gateman told Harry, who was twelve years old and couldn't ever remember not working at the lumber yard. Harry ran into the man building and told Evelyn.

Evelyn knocked on Smith's office door and without waiting for any response opened it. The heavy oak felt weightless on its oiled hinges.

Washington Smith was standing by the window, an empty glass in his hand.

He turned.

'Who are they?' he asked.

'Texas Rangers,' she said. 'Seven of them. One's a woman.'

'A woman?'

'That's what Harry said.'

'Texas Rangers, huh.'

It wasn't a question, but Evelyn nodded anyway.

'Tell Harry to tell them I'll be down.'

'You don't want me to show them up?'

Smith cast a quick look at the other two men in the room.

He looked back at Evelyn.

'I'll come down in a minute.'

Evelyn closed the door.

Smith looked at Abraham.

'How do you feel about killing Texas Rangers?'

* * *

The Texas Ranger called Hero Villemont eased his horse between Jim and Leon's horses. He pulled a slim leather wallet from inside his jacket.

He looked at Leon. 'Smoke?'

Leon smiled and said, 'No, thank you. My lungs . . . '

Hero looked at him.

'Nothing fresh air and milk won't cure,' Leon said.

Hero smiled and turned to Jim.

'Would you like one?' Hero had a faint French accent.

'I used to,' Jim said. 'Gave it up for ten years, and no matter how hard I tried I couldn't get started again.'

'Well you two are really something,' Hero said. He turned to Rosalie. 'Would the pretty lady like a cigarette?'

Rosalie smiled. 'Why not?'

Hero handed a thin rolled cigarette to Rosalie. He flicked a Lucifer into life and leaned across towards her. He lit her cigarette.

'So why?' he asked. 'Why are you here? All of you, I mean.'

Rosalie breathed out smoke.

'This is where we've been led,' she said. 'This is where it ends.'

'What ends?' Hero asked.

'Everything,' Rosalie said.

★ ★ ★

'No way,' Charles Beecher said. 'It doesn't matter whether there's one or seven. No way. No killing. Not Rangers.'

'So what do you suggest?' Smith said. 'Talk nicely to them?'

'You don't even know what they want?'

'We know they . . . ' Smith tapped his fingers on the photos of Jim Jackson and Leon Winters, ' . . . were in Leyton. We know that Anderson likely mouthed off. Probably about us. So they know about

205

you and I. There was a woman with them. Isn't that right?' He looked at Abraham.

'That's right,' Abraham said. 'A pretty woman.'

'There's a woman with those riders down at the gate. It's them. And you know why they're here.'

'So you're going to kill them? All of them?'

'It's an idea.'

'You're drunk.'

'What do you suggest? Go out there with our hands up?'

'You think if these men disappear they won't send more? You think they haven't discussed it? Written it down on a report or a plan somewhere?'

'Seems to me you fellows don't know what you want,' Abraham said. He stood up. 'I'm heading down to the saw mill. I'll talk to your fellow, Ike Landreth, like you said Mr Smith. You want me to kill any of these fellows you just walk them on down to the saw mill. If nothing happens in thirty minutes I'll assume you're both in jail.'

'No,' Beecher said. 'Let me talk to them. You'll just make it worse.'

'And if you fellows don't pay me,' Abraham said. 'It'll be worse still.'

★ ★ ★

'Someone coming,' Will Baker said.

The man was wearing a dark suit, with a vest and a gold watch chain. He looked warm. His shaven cheeks were red. He walked out of the office, not too fast, and came towards the gate. He looked up at Will Baker.

'My name is Charles Beecher. I believe you want to see me?'

'You and Mr Smith.'

'Mr Smith isn't here right now. Would you care to come up to my office?'

'Where's Smith?'

'It's a big site.'

'He's here?'

'Somewhere.'

Will Baker looked at the man who had been manning the gate when they had arrived.

'You know Mr Smith?'

'Yes, of course.'

Baker turned to two of his men. 'Fellows, you go with . . . Sorry what was your name, sir?'

'Bolton. Bolton, sir.'

'Fellows, you go with Bolton and you find Mr Smith and bring him back here. Back to Mr Beecher's office.'

'What's this all about?' Beecher asked, his cheeks even redder now, a tremble in his voice.

'You recognize these fellers?' Baker asked. He nodded at Jim Jackson and Leon Winters.

'No.'

'See, that's the trouble. Folks like you, you don't actually look people in the eye when you do them wrong.'

'I don't understand.'

'You will,' Baker said. He turned to Hero Villemont. 'H, you just wait here. Anyone looks like they're making a run for it . . . Well, you know.'

'Yessir,' Hero said and winked at Rosalie.

Baker looked back at Beecher. 'Let's go up to your office then, and wait for Mr Smith.'

★ ★ ★

Evelyn brought in a large pot of English tea, on a tray, with bone china cups, a small jug of cream, and a silver bowl of sugar lumps. She set the tray down on the polished mahogany table. That table was, Jim thought, almost as big and empty as the plains not far north. Beecher tapped his finger tips on the table top. The table reflected them back better than many a mirror. Beecher's hand shook when he picked up one of the cups from the tray, and the cup rattled against its saucer.

'You might be interested in these,' Will Baker said to Jim.

Jim took a couple of steps over to where Will was looking at several photographs piled on the sideboard. His own photograph. Leon's, too. And the others.

'What the hell,' Jim said.

He turned, and was just about to ask

Beecher why he and Smith had these photographs when Leon started coughing blood and, simultaneously, they heard a volley of gunshots from outside in the yard.

13

Ike Landreth thought how easy killing was when you had someone like Abraham telling you what to do, where to stand, and when to do it. Abraham's voice was low and serene, his body still and tall and commanding. His beard almost biblical. No matter how scared Ike was of pulling the trigger the way Abraham had ordered him to, he was even more scared of disobeying the man. Hell, he wouldn't have disobeyed the Greek either, if he had still been alive. And no doubt the Greek would have had him shoot the Texas Ranger, too. That was the way with these people. Killing was easy.

Washington Smith had come down to the vast saw mill a minute before. He'd told the men, all of them to clear out. 'Leave the saws and the engines running,' he told them. 'This won't take a moment.'

He'd been carrying a shotgun. A real

211

shiny Winchester with a lever action.

One of the men, a Polish fellow that Ike knew only as Slav, had looked at that Winchester, and he had looked at Abraham and he'd said to Washington Smith. 'Do you need some help, boss?'

Which was how it came to be that Washington Smith was standing there, looking at the spinning blades as if taking a note of how slick his operation was, with Abraham leaning against the brick base of one of the great steam engines, and Ike himself behind the second engine, with that shiny Winchester now in his trembling hands. Behind one of the big circular saw blades was the Slav and two of his European cousins, and over where the main water tank was were two more fellows, a Canadian and a Mexican, and they had guns too, although their guns were still in their waistbands.

'How do you know this is where they'll look?' Ike asked Smith.

'They'll look everywhere,' Smith said, his voice sounding slightly strange to Ike. There was a hint of a slur to the words but at the same time they rang out hard and clear, as if the tenseness and gravity of the moment was overriding the alcohol that Smith had clearly drunk. 'And when they get here. This is where they'll find me.'

It was only a few minutes later that Bolton Hardy came wandering along with two mean-looking fellers behind him. Bolton was smiling as if he knew exactly what he was doing, but then Bolton was always smiling. That's why Smith left him on the gate duty most of the time. The two mean looking men were both holding rifles. They walked a few feet behind Bolton and they were turning this way and that as they walked, looking left, right, and behind, fingers real close to the triggers of those rifles. They had on dark coats and dark hats, and it was hard to see their eyes. But the way they walked — they were standing straight and they held themselves as if they knew that whatever was coming they could handle it.

Bolton walked them right up to the

edge of the sawing area. There was a high roof over two very long and wide saw benches. The benches were long enough to hold a whole pine log two times over. The great wheeled blades were halfway along the benches. Metal rods linked to the steam engines turned with a high whine and the saw blades spun round and round, faster or slower depending on how the operator set the pressure and the gears. The logs were pulled slowly forwards with chains and ropes, which themselves were controlled by smaller steam engines. The room was noisy and hot — despite being open to the breeze on all sides.

'There he is,' Bolton said. 'That's Mr Smith right there.'

The two men followed Bolton's pointing finger.

They were just about level with the left cutting blade. They were on the outside of the building, the sun illuminating them as if a clear white light was aimed directly on them.

One of the men started to lower his

rifle in the general direction of Smith. The other, still on his guard, continued his surveillance of just about everything.

'Gentlemen,' Smith said, smiling, stepping away from the bench on which he'd been leaning.

'You're needed in the office,' the first of the men said, the one who's gun was half lowered.

'Shoot them,' Smith said quietly.

Ike stepped out from his hiding place, lowering his own gun — Smith's shotgun — levering a cartridge into the breech, when Abraham's guns blazed, one in each hand. The Slav and both of his cousins stepped from behind the saw blade and they had guns in their hands, too. They all fired pretty much simultaneously. The Mexican drew as well, but Ike didn't know if he actually pulled the trigger. Saws were whining and the steam engines were hissing and banging and a furnace door was open on one of them and the heat was burning Ike's legs and those two men … One moment they were standing, full of confidence, albeit a little wary, looking around for trouble, and the next moment there were clouds of blood and flesh exploding from their necks and their backs as the bullets smashed into their bodies and burst outwards into that white light in a red mist. The two men, as if one, crumpled to the ground, a surprised look in their fading eyes.

And killing was that easy.

★ ★ ★

'Don't move!' Will Baker yelled, and Jim Jackson had no idea if the Ranger was talking to Charles Beecher, or to him, Leon, and Rosalie.

Leon was still doubled over from the coughing fit, a string of blood suspended from his lips.

Jim caught his friend's gaze, nodded, and hoped that the understanding between them was enough, then he raced down the stairs behind Baker.

The building entrance was on the main thoroughfare of the yard, the gates and their horses to their right, the long railway platform in front of them. A train of flat wagons, most still piled high with lumber, stood at the platform. To their left, beyond the building they'd just stepped out from, the thoroughfare opened up into a wide space, with the massive saw mill over to the right beyond the end of the platform. Jim Jackson saw piles of cut wood, steam engines, several hand coal trucks, water tanks, and lying in the sun light about fifty yards ahead of them, over by the mill, the bodies of Will Baker's men.

'Son of a bitch,' Baker said. He had his revolver in his hand.

'Get down, boss!' Hero Villemont yelled. 'There's dozens of them!'

Villemont was crouching by one of the flatbed wagons across the yard.

'Warren and Gid are both dead, boss,' Villemont said.

Jim Jackson was in the doorway behind Will Baker. The wound in his shoulder was burning with the sudden exertion, but adrenaline was keeping most of the pain at bay. He held his own gun — Sam McRea's gun — in his hand.

The thoroughfare was deserted. Engines still clanked and there was a hiss of steam from the locomotive but there was no one in sight, not even the gateman.

'What happened?' Baker said, he had darted out of the doorway and was crouched behind a large pile of wooden packing cases, the top one of which was stencilled Chicago Steam Co. 'They might not be dead.'

'It was like a volley from the army,' Villemont said. 'Must have been six or seven people waiting for them.'

'I need to know for sure.'

'Don't go down there, boss. I'll go.'

'No. I'll — '

'I can get down there behind the train,' Villemont called. Even as he said the words he was stepping out from behind the cover of the wagon, crouching low, and running alongside the train, each flatbed wagon in turn offering him cover as he neared the saw mill.

Without looking at Jim Jackson, Baker said, 'I told you to stay put upstairs.'

'We can cover him,' Jim said. 'I'll get the opposite side of the train. They must be down there in the saw mill.'

'If you get killed the paperwork's going to be horrendous,' Baker said.

Villemont was twenty yards along the train now, edging towards the locomotive, which sat quietly smoking and steaming. The whole area was still deserted, seemingly devoid of life. Just the two bodies of the Texas Rangers lying in the sun where they had been ambushed.

Jim stepped out of the doorway and raced across the open thoroughfare to shelter against the flat wagons where Villemont had been twenty seconds before. He looked back at Baker. The Texas Ranger nodded at him and Jim saw him rising up from behind the Chicago boxes. Then Jim turned, climbed between two wagons and started running towards the area from where the hidden men had shot down the Rangers.

Even before the echoes of the gunshots had stopped ringing in his ears Washington Smith told Abraham, and anyone else who was listening, that they knew what to do. That he expected them to finish the job. Then he turned and walked as fast as his fifty-year-old legs would carry him across the yard and around the back of the main building. He spied a few workers peering out from the various hiding places they had rushed to when the first bullets had started flying. Some were peering through windows, others were behind sheds and piles of timber.

'Just stay out of it,' he called, waving his hands, palm down. 'It'll be over in a minute.'

He went through the back door of the office, and from a cupboard on the wall, he grabbed a shotgun and a box of shells. He cracked open the gun as he walked through the office where a few of his administration workers looked at him, their faces pale and ghostlike in the dark interior.

'Stay still,' he said. 'It's all in hand.'

He fumbled two shells from the box and slotted them into the gun barrels as he strode past his own telegraph room and up the back-stairs, his feet sounding loud on the uncarpeted wooden stairs.

Everything felt unreal. That singular blast of how many guns? Six? Seven? Those Texas Rangers literally disappearing. One moment carefully looking around and the next crumpling as if they were nothing but screwed up paper bags thrown on a fire. It was almost dreamlike. Maybe a drunken memory that you weren't sure had happened. But it had happened and he now felt invincible. He found himself smiling. This was only the beginning of it. But that was OK. He'd finish what he had to right here and now. Then they could clear up. Hell, within ten minutes with the steam engines and furnaces and saws they had here those men, all of them — including the woman — would just disappear, truly disappear. Maybe then he'd take a ride into town. Talk to Commissioners Reynolds and Johnson. And then what? Hell, he'd worry about that once this situation was taken care of.

And this situation included Charles Beecher.

Beecher was the only other one who knew the truth.

He snapped the barrels of the gun into place and he pushed open the door to his outer office, smiled at Evelyn, who was standing by her window looking out, her face pale.

Then he burst into his own office.

* * *

Jim Jackson made it as far as the locomotive. He ran through the steam, past the smell of hot oil and he crouched low and pressed himself up against the metal buffers that marked the end of the line. He glanced to the left. There was no sign of Villemont. He must still be behind the other side of the locomotive. From here Jim could more clearly see the bodies of the two Rangers. They were dead for sure. They lay still and blood pooled around them like dark growing shadows. Jim's hands were slick with fear and his shoulder now sent pulses of pain across his neck and the top of his back. He tried to control his breathing, keep the sound of the air rushing into his burning lungs quiet. At least the engines in the area were still turning, the pipes clanking, valves hissing, a furnace somewhere roaring. Long rods that linked from engines to saw blades were spinning although the blades themselves were still. He could smell burning, coal and fire and gunpowder. He was just about to yell out to Villemont and Baker, wherever they were, to get out of there, that he could clearly see the Rangers were dead, when he noticed the three men standing behind one of the massive circular saw blades. The inside of the saw room was dark. The men were just silhouettes, but silhouettes with guns. Another shape became a man as he shifted his weight in the blackness alongside a steam engine cylinder.

Then Jim's eyes adjusted and there were more. Men behind the second saw blade, men by the steam engines, men over there by the water tank.

Jim clenched his teeth, locking the warning inside.

Villemont broke cover to his left, racing over to the bodies of the two Rangers.

And all hell broke loose.

★ ★ ★

Rosalie Robertson had one arm around Leon's shoulders, when the man with the shotgun burst into the room. The man was wearing a suit jacket with matching trousers and a tie. The tie was loose and there was dirt on his white shirt. He came through the door and in the same movement lowered the shotgun so that its double barrels pointed forwards, those barrels wavering this way and that as he took in the situation.

'Wash', what the hell!' the one called Charles Beecher said. He'd been by the window, looking out. Rosalie thought that he had been quietly praying.

When Jim and Will Baker had run outside following the sounds of the gunshots a few minutes before Leon had said to Beecher, 'You're staying here. Don't move.' And he'd drawn his gun to reinforce the point. But then he'd started coughing and choking again, and it was so violent that he couldn't do anything but lean over and spit and dribble and expel long tendrils of thick blood. Even with the gunshots outside and Beecher — one of the two men that had started all of this hell all of those years ago — in the room with him the dark thing inside his lungs was stronger and he couldn't resist the pain as it dug it's claws into his insides. So Rosalie had drawn her own gun, a Colt 45 she'd been wearing since the days when they had been hiding out after Leon's prison break. She put her arm around Leon's shoulders whilst he retched and she told him that it would be all right, and she kept her gun aimed at Beecher. And now here was someone else, bursting into the room, his eyes red, bloodshot and crazy, the gun pointing at Beecher, then at Leon and finally, the man's eyes focussing on her and the gun in her hand, the barrels swung that final inch towards her and the man squeezed one of the dual triggers.

* * *

The darkness in the saw mill lit up like the sky over the western mountains in the wildest of lightning storms. A shotgun, several revolvers, another shotgun. Flames exploded from barrels, the sound of gunfire rebounded off the metal roof and Hero Villemont screamed, albeit briefly, as bullet after bullet slammed into him, lifted him off his feet, and deposited him on top of one of the very Rangers he had come to check for signs of life.

In the darkness Jim stood up, the gun in his hand. He didn't recall making the decision to draw or fire. It just happened. It was who he was these days. After everything that had happened he was a killer now.

His gun blazed. Taking the men by the saw blade by surprise. One, two. All three of them. Then Jim turning, firing by instinct and hearing the man by the steam engine cry out. Several men shot back at him. He saw the flames from their guns, heard the cartridges exploding and the whistle of bullets in the air. But he was low again now, and although he heard bullets clanking off metalwork, nothing hit him.

Now there were more shots, and a man by the water tank yelled out, fell backwards, and was still. Jim Jackson realized that Will Baker was there too, standing by the locomotive, ploughing bullets into the darkness, picking out the men from their muzzle flashes as they'd shot at Jim.

Jim took the opportunity to reload, and by the time he'd done so, Baker had stopped shooting, and no one was firing back.

Baker retreated behind the locomotive and Jim Jackson stayed crouched down at the platform edge.

He held his breath.

Nothing moved.

Then he heard another shot. Maybe a shotgun blast. And another. And then a series of gunshots that sounded like a string of fire crackers going off.

They were all coming from the office block back over to his left. The block where he'd left Leon and Rosalie.

★ ★ ★

There had been a time, months before, when Leon had moved that quickly to save her and Jim's lives. Then it had been to drive a bread knife deep into the guts of a man who had been about to kill them all. His action that day had saved them all, himself included. This time, she knew it was the last thing he would ever do. It took all his strength, all he had left, which she knew wasn't much.

He knew it, too.

He'd always known it.

The man — Washington Smith — was

grimacing and there was fury in his face. From outside there was the sound of gunfire, so much gunfire, that it might have been two armies engaging. Rosalie felt her insides twisting up in terror and confusion and fear for Jim Jackson. Then Smith squeezed the shotgun trigger and nothing happened. He yelled at them for being interfering lowlifes and he squeezed the trigger harder, and in that brief instance Leon Winters rolled out of her arms, the arms that had been comforting him as the tuberculosis tore at his insides, and he somehow swivelled so that he was in front of her. The shotgun roared and the blast of it picked them both up and slammed them back against the wall. She felt a hundred burning wounds in her arms and her legs and her hair. There was warm horrible wetness all around and she couldn't breathe because the air had been knocked out of her. Leon was on top of her. He wasn't breathing either and she knew, just knew with a certainty and a knowledge that was the hardest knowledge that had ever come to her, that Leon was dead. That never again would he struggle to breathe, that his days of agonising lung-burning coughing were over, that he wouldn't need the clean air and the vegetables and the milk that Doctor Koch had prescribed, that he would have all the rest in the world. Damn this world, but at least he was with Charlotte and Harvey, whom he'd spent so many late nights beneath the stars talking about.

She heard someone — Beecher — begging.

'Please,' he was saying. 'Please.' Then: 'Mary. What about Mary?'

Another shotgun blast rocked the room. In the silence that followed, the silence caused by shockwaves dulling her hearing, she managed to gather in a lungful of air and she squirmed from beneath Leon's ruined body and she rose up, covered in Leon's blood.

Washington Smith, standing over the body of Charles Beecher, smoke still coming from the barrels of his shotgun, looked over at her. His eyes widened.

'This one's for Leon,' she said.

And she shot Washington Smith, over and over again, until her gun was empty.

* * *

Ike Landreth still hadn't fired a shot. Killing was easy. He'd seen that. He'd seen that so many times in the last few minutes that he knew it to be an unquestionable truth. But it was easy in the same way that one of the girls — he forgot her name, Daisy probably — could play tunes on the piano over in the bar. She could make music burst out of that piano like it was the easiest thing in the world. She could stand up and make music and she could shake her chest and dance and flirt and make music. He'd even seen a fellow pouring wine down her throat as she played. It was easy. But only if you knew how.

He was still crouching behind one of the engines. They — the bearded fellow, and the Slav and his brothers and the Mexican and all of them — had blown away three Texas Rangers as if it had been the most natural thing in the world. But then out of the blue someone — two people — had suddenly started blasting them.

And they were all dead. Or so it seemed.

No one was moving, least of all him. In fact he wondered if he'd ever move again.

'Jackson, you all right?' somebody called.

'Yes. You?'

'Yes. Back-up. Retreat, my friend.'

'That shooting upstairs . . . '

'I know. I've got it covered. Let's go.'

Ike Landreth's legs gave way then and he sank to the floor behind the steam engine and without realising it, he began to weep again, just like last time there had been killing.

* * *

The woman with red hair was standing in the doorway. Her shoulders were heaving and she had a hand over her mouth.

'He shot them,' she said. 'He came in with a gun and he shot them.' A sob caught in her throat.

Jim pushed by the woman.

The room was hazy with gun smoke. The smell of cordite thickened the air. But there was also a horrible metallic tang in the atmosphere, so strong it was almost a taste rather than a smell.

Two men lay on the floor just inside the door, by the window.

Rosalie was standing against the far wall, a revolver in her hand. The wall behind her was covered in blood and at her feet was Leon.

'Rosalie,' Jim said. Then he saw Leon. 'My God.'

He rushed over to her, held her wrists, looked into her eyes.

'Are you OK?'

For a moment it was as if she didn't recognize him. Her eyes struggled to focus and when they did they filled with moisture and tears spilled down and mixed with the blood that was on her cheeks.

Behind him he heard Will Baker saying.

'They're dead. The two of them.'

'Are you hurt?' Jim asked Rosalie. There was blood running from her hairline.

She shook her head.

Her eyes were magnified beneath the tears and she looked so terrified, but worse than that, it was as if those eyes had witnessed something that had forever changed what lay behind them.

'I'm OK,' she said slowly. Then: 'Leon.'

'We have to go,' Will Baker said. 'Now.'

Jim looked into Rosalie's eyes. Then, his heart breaking, he tore his gaze away and looked down at her feet. He let go of Rosalie's wrists and he crouched down.

'He saved my life,' Rosalie said.

Jim rolled Leon over onto his back.

'Leon,' he said. 'Leon.'

But he knew there would be no response. His friend was almost unrecognizable. The shotgun blast had been too close. It had torn him open. He wasn't breathing.

'Leon,' Jim said again.

'He's dead,' Will Baker said. 'Come on. We'll be back for him.'

In the doorway the red-haired woman said, 'He was crazy, I don't mean just today. These last few weeks. Crazier and crazier.'

Jim Jackson felt Will Baker's hand on his elbow.

'Come on, my friend. We'll be back before the sun goes down. I promise. But right now we have to go.'

Jim Jackson looked down at Leon again.

Then he allowed himself to be pulled away from his friend. Will Baker led them down the stairs and into the fresh air, into the blinding sunshine. Further along the yard people were stirring, coming out of their hiding places, their offices, and their sheds. A steam valve was shrieking, pistons were clanking, and horses were nickering. Someone somewhere said 'What the hell happened?' and Will

Baker pushed Jim and Rosalie towards their own horses, which were standing along from the huge gate to their right.

'Ride,' he said.

Then Jim Jackson heard, behind him, Rosalie say, 'Abraham.'

The bearded man was standing opposite them.

'Rosalie,' he said.

He stood tall and still. He had two guns on his hips, and despite the heat he still had his coat on.

Jim Jackson looked at Abraham.

Their eyes met.

The gunman's hands hovered close to his revolvers. Jim felt his own hands tense. He recalled the moment when this man had thrown one of those very guns to him way back up in Leyton. The man had saved his life.

'We need to go,' Will Baker said.

Abraham nodded, almost imperceptibly. A tiny smile crossed his lips.

Then Jim Jackson turned away and he, Rosalie, and Will Baker leapt on their horses and raced out of the gate and away from Beecher and Smith's lumber yard.

14

That evening Will Baker returned to Beecher and Smith's yard. This time twenty-seven Texas Rangers rode with him. Every Texas Ranger that was in rounding up distance went. Not a single bullet was fired on that second occasion. The lumber yard was still running, the steam engines still smoking, and the saw blades spinning. The locomotive that Jim Jackson and Hero Villemont had hidden behind was gone, and there was already a stack of lumber awaiting the next train out. But there was an air of confusion and sadness, a darkness and a heaviness, around the camp. It seemed that people walked slowly and said little, and what they said, they said quietly.

Nobody wanted to fight.

The bodies had been taken to a large shed where tools were kept, and there they had been covered in canvas sheets.

Three Texas Rangers, Leon Winters,

Beecher and Smith, a Mexican, three Europeans, and a Canadian.

In Washington Smith's office, the red-head, who turned out to be called Evelyn, was still scrubbing blood from the floor and walls. In that office Will Baker found the photographs of all the members of the train-robbing gang of which Jim Jackson and Leon Smith had once been a part. He found a map of Texas on the wall, and there were blue pins in the map that he discovered later represented the camps where Commissioners Reynolds and Johnson would make sure the vast majority of leased prisoners were allocated.

Reynolds and Johnson had been paid well, mightily well, by Beecher and Smith. And the next morning, exhausted, but determined to see it through, Will Baker had personally arrested both men in their Austin mansions, full of porcelains and paintings, polished floors, servants, and outrage.

It would take weeks, long weeks in which the two politicians demanded that

Will Baker be suspended, be fired, heck even be hanged for treason! The politicians called in favours and demanded to see the Governor. They threatened the Texas Rangers with disbandment and for a while they appeared to be gaining enough support and momentum that Will Baker wondered if they might get away with it.

But little by little, diary by diary, notebook by notebook, and ledger by ledger, the truth came out. Signatures on lease approvals sending prisoners to prison lumber camps owned by Beecher and Smith were mapped against prisoner-allocation voting records — records that showed two-to-one voting every time, with Reynolds and Johnson always out-voting the third man on the Prison Board. The third commissioner had changed several times over the years, but Reynolds and Johnson stayed put. Now that the truth was starting to be uncovered some of those other Board members came forward and admitted they'd had suspicions about what was going on.

Bank payment records were subpoenaed. The investigation would go on for months, but towards the end of it, Reynolds and Johnson started to talk about making deals, about giving up names of leasing camp captains, if maybe they could escape with lesser sentences.

No deals were offered.

Not long after the two men had been sent to Huntsville to serve out sentences that Will Baker thought far too short, legislation was proposed and passed that saw the end of the prisoner leasing programme.

'It came too late for all of us,' Jim Jackson said to Will Baker over coffee in the mess room of the Texas Rangers' barracks.

Will Baker said, 'At least it came. No change comes easy. But, my friend, at least you made a difference.'

* * *

They buried Leon Winters in the yard of a small, and fairly young, church out on the west side of Austin. The church was out beyond the edge of the growing city.

'He wouldn't want to be buried in town,' Rosalie said. 'He liked the open spaces.'

'I'm not sure he would want to be buried in Texas,' Jim said. 'After all that Texas did to him.'

They'd talked about trying to find where Charlotte and Harvey were buried. That's where he should lie really, they'd both agreed. With his family. But they had no way of finding where Leon's wife and son lay, and even as autumn progressed, the days were too warm to leave a body unburied.

Jim and Rosalie, Roberta and Andrew Beaumont, Doctor Koch, Will Baker and several of his Ranger colleagues stood at Leon's graveyard that day and Jim tried to say in faltering and tear-laden words how such a fine man had no place in such a cruel world and how every breath in Leon's life had been taken for someone else, and Rosalie had said that even his last breath, his last action, had been taken so that she may live.

A year later, she and Jim would name their first son Leon.

'After my best friend ever,' Jim said.

★ ★ ★

Throughout the months of the Reynolds and Johnson trials Rosalie stayed with Roberta. Jim Jackson took a room at a small hotel just a few streets away. He found it strange to be able to walk the streets of Austin without the fear of arrest.

The city was expanding — or so it felt — daily. There were electric lights in his hotel room and sometimes Jim just flicked them on and off in wonderment. It was strange not to sleep in the open, beneath the stars, and it was hard not to have Rosalie by his side at night.

'It's just for a few weeks,' she'd said. 'Whilst we decide what to do.'

And what were they to do?

He was an eastern boy who had only ventured west to make a quick fortune in order to marry the girl of his dreams. He had indeed made a fortune, but it was long gone, as were too many years. He'd found another girl — this one even beyond his dreams. He'd lived through hell and he'd come out the other side.

But what now?

Each day he stayed in the city it felt like it would be harder to leave. Not because he didn't want to. But because of Rosalie.

The day he'd met her she had been on a train travelling into Austin. How could he take her away from the soft clothes and the comfortable beds, the tram cars and the running water and the electric lights? How could he have her sleep beneath the stars again? Especially with winter coming on.

And why would they do that? What would they do *out there?*

He'd been an engineering student once, a very long time ago.

'You could do that,' she'd said to him, in a café on Brazos Street. 'There must be a thousand opportunities for an engineer in Austin.'

She was right. He'd enjoyed being an engineer, too. Although he'd never really got beyond the books. But it no longer appealed the way it once had. Something had changed. Out there, beneath the open sky, on horse-back. There was freedom. It was being your own man. It was making a difference, not through designing a way of making a steam engine more efficient or a building stronger, but by standing up for what was right. By facing down evil.

There'd been excitement in Rosalie's eyes when she had been talking of him being an engineer. She'd been wearing a nice coat, a blue knitted coat. A woman's coat.

How could he take all that away from her?

He recalled her telling him, so long ago now — or at least it felt like that because so much had happened since — how she had travelled west, had her share of adventures and, having got them out of her system returned to the city. That's when he had first met her. On her return to the city. He had yanked her out of that. Taken her back to the wilderness. Taken her through things that no woman should ever have to face.

Now she was in the city once again and he saw the excitement in her eyes when she imagined a role for him there.

Sometimes he thought of the town of Parker's Crossing where he had first emerged from the darkness of his prison years. For a while Parker's Crossing had been home. He wondered if it could be again. Maybe that was the answer. He'd promised his friends there that one day he would go back — and it was a promise he would keep. But was it possible, if not likely, that Parker's Crossing would be as civilized as Austin soon? Who knows, maybe it already was? And that was the other thing. In his bones he knew that there was a time coming when no one would sleep beneath the stars any more. Things were changing too fast. The world was changing.

He thought upon all of this, but most

of all he thought about being a killer.

He no longer wore his gun, although it was still with his small pile of belongings back in his hotel room. The nightmares and the guilt were receding — partly because of time, but mostly because he was able to talk such things through with Rosalie. She had killed Washington Smith and she seemed to take it a lot better than he did. They talked for hours about how and why he felt so guilty and slowly the anguish eased.

But it didn't change the fact.

He was a killer, not an engineer, and no amount of flicking electric lights on and off made him feel at home.

* * *

Will Baker said, 'Walk with me, my friend.'

They were down by the railroad tracks. As far as the eye could see were pens of cattle. The noise settled over them as they walked — the lowing of cows and bulls, horses neighing and bickering, cowboys yelling and laughing, the occasional crack of a whip, dogs barking, the hiss of steam and a whistle from a locomotive. The smells too, steam and coal smoke, cattle and wet straw, tobacco smoke, body heat from men and animals.

'It's like a different world down here, isn't it?' Baker said. He turned and looked back up the hill into town, at the great Capitol building construction, the houses and shops, vast hotels and offices, squares and avenues, stretching out in all directions.

'It's like . . . ' Jim Jackson tried to find the words for what he was feeling. 'It's like it used to be,' he said.

'I know what you mean,' Baker said. 'Nothing stays the same. But . . . '

'But what?'

'It's still like it right here, isn't it? I mean, *here's* the proof. Right in front of our eyes.'

'I guess so.'

'And if it can still be like it here, in the capital. Well, I guess it can be like it anywhere. For a long while yet, anyway.'

'What are you saying?'

'You don't know what to do, do you?'

'It's that obvious?'

'Uh-huh. Rosalie said something, too.'

'Did she now?'

'She's worried.'

'She likes it here.'

'Who wouldn't? Don't you?'

'I . . . I guess so. I just feel that I don't fit.'

'All these students and business types,' Will Baker said.

'And engineers.'

'Engineers?'

'Rosalie thinks I'd make a good engineer.'

'There's still a lot of cowboys around,' Will Baker said. 'Look at them.'

'I'm no good with cattle.'

'But you're good with a gun. You're brave. More than brave. You're courageous and you're determined to do the right thing, no matter how hard that thing is.'

Jim Jackson stopped walking.

'What are you saying?'

'You don't want to be an engineer and you don't want to be a cowboy. How do you fancy being a Texas Ranger?'

★ ★ ★

Will Baker was best man and Roberta Robertson was bridesmaid. They were married in the same church where Leon Winters was buried. They lived in a small house just along from Roberta's house and a year later Leon Jackson was born.

Jim Jackson, Texas Ranger, wore Sam McRae's gun for many more years. Once or twice he even had to draw it in anger, which he did with a lightning speed that came naturally to him. But he never had to kill another man.

His reputation and the legend of Gentleman Jim Jackson went before him.

We do hope that you have enjoyed reading this large print book.

Did you know that all of our titles are available for purchase?

We publish a wide range of high quality large print books including:
Romances, Mysteries, Classics
General Fiction
Non Fiction and Westerns

Special interest titles available in large print are:
The Little Oxford Dictionary
Music Book, Song Book
Hymn Book, Service Book

Also available from us courtesy of Oxford University Press:
Young Readers' Dictionary
(large print edition)
Young Readers' Thesaurus
(large print edition)

For further information or a free brochure, please contact us at:
Ulverscroft Large Print Books Ltd.,
The Green, Bradgate Road, Anstey,
Leicester, LE7 7FU, England.
Tel: (00 44) **0116 236 4325**
Fax: (00 44) **0116 234 0205**

*Other titles in the
Linford Western Library:*

REMARQUE'S LAW

Will DuRey

Ben Joyner has no argument with the people who settled on the grassland near Pecos, but other cattlemen have long considered the range their own domain. Ben's boss Gus Remarque believes a dollar a day buys not only a man's labour, but his loyalty too. When that loyalty might involve killing or being killed, Ben wants to wash his hands of the dispute. So he quits the ranch and rides east. But then a strong-willed woman alters his plans . . .